Like father, like daug...
bitterly at first sight ...
beautiful Diane de V...
was a traitor, he is de...
Comte de Verette will ever marry into the Moreton
family, whatever steps he has to take to prevent
it . . .

But surely there must be a better way to foil Diane's
part in the attempted rescue of Napoleon from St
Helena—and save his brother from her clutches—
than marrying her himself?

By the same author in Masquerade

TRAITOR'S HEIR

JASMINE CRESSWELL

MILLS & BOON LIMITED
15–16 BROOK'S MEWS
LONDON W1A 1DR

First published in Great Britain 1984
by Mills & Boon Limited

© Jasmine Cresswell 1984

Australian copyright 1984
Philippine copyright 1984
This edition 1984

ISBN 0 263 74931 2

Set in 11 on 12 pt Linotron Times
04–1284–55,000

Photoset by Rowland Phototypesetting Ltd
Bury St Edmunds, Suffolk
Made and printed in Great Britain by
Cox & Wyman Ltd, Reading

CHAPTER
ONE

THE COMTE de Verette's body lay on the gilded bed, draped with a golden silk cover. Two servants, elderly retainers who had escaped with their master's family from France, stood in respectful silence at its foot. Their heads were bowed and they each held a lighted candle, but their faces showed no sign of overwhelming grief. The Comte had valued his servants for their practical skills, not for the warmth of their characters or for their long years of faithful service.

Diane de Verette tore her gaze away from the servants and turned back to look again at her father. She searched his pallid face intently as if now, after twenty years of incomprehension, she might finally learn to understand him. It was a foolish hope, of course. In death, as in life, her father's features remained inscrutable. His mouth was unsmiling, his lips tightly compressed. His nostrils seemed pinched, as though to indicate his contempt for the petty inefficiencies and muddled emotions of humankind. Altogether, Diane reflected, it was not the face of a man who tolerated fools gladly.

She reached out hesitantly to caress the delicate,

aristocratic line of her father's jaw. The skin was icy cold, but what else had she expected? Two tears trickled down her cheeks and lost themselves in the frill of black lace at her throat. She had so desperately wanted her father to love her, and now it was finally and irrevocably too late.

She pulled out a handkerchief and brushed away the tears, knowing her father would have scorned them. She wished that—just for once—she could do something that was exactly in accordance with his wishes. Unfortunately, she had no idea what his wishes would have been. The Comte de Verette had not been in the habit of confiding his thoughts to anybody, least of all to his only child.

Diane had long since learned to accept the Comte's utter coldness, although she had never managed to abandon her useless struggle to please him. A cynical half-smile from her father had always seemed more valuable than the most lyrical praise from one of her many suitors. She understood why her father could not like her, and accepted the fact of her guilt. She was the perpetrator of a double crime: her mother had died in giving her life, and she was merely a female, not the son and heir the Comte had longed for.

One of the old maidservants had confided in a rare moment of intimacy that the Comte had loved his beautiful wife to the point of madness. He had never, the maid asserted, recovered from the shock of her death. Diane listened to the story and tried to reconcile the image of her father as a passionate lover with the restrained and calculating man she knew. She found the task impossible. It was difficult to believe that the Comte had ever loved anybody at all; it was impossible to accept that he had once loved his countess to the point of madness.

The entry of a young footman interrupted Diane's disjointed thoughts. 'Mr Thomas Baker is here to pay his respects, mademoiselle.'

She hesitated for no more than a second. 'Please ask him to come in.'

Mr Baker was a lawyer by profession and he looked very much the part. He was dressed in neat black, his linen plain but impeccably white and his expression exactly the proper blend of respect and sorrow. Mr Baker's facial expressions, Diane thought irritably, were *always* the perfect fit for the occasion.

'My dear Mademoiselle de Verette, this is indeed a mournful day.'

'Yes.' She removed her hand from his limp grasp. 'It was good of you to call, Mr Baker.'

'Not at all. I am, after all, the Comte's man of affairs. I flatter myself that no other human being held the Comte in higher esteem than I. Certainly nobody here in London knew him as well as I did.'

Mr Baker's glance slid over the golden-draped body in a quick, sharp scrutiny. Diane had the oddest impression that he was actually reassuring himself that the Comte was really dead. 'Tragic, tragic, and so sudden an end to such a healthy existence.' Mr Baker made a vague snuffling noise before lifting his spectacles and wiping a black-bordered linen handkerchief across his eyes. Diane could not help noticing that it returned to his pocket without any visible sign of being dampened by tears. Not for the first time in her life, she cursed her acute powers of observation. Too much perception, she had discovered, made the London social round exceptionally difficult.

'My dear Mademoiselle de Verette, may I so far intrude upon your grief as to solicit a few moments of your time away from the precious mortal remains of your beloved Papa?'

'Do you mean, Mr Baker, that you wish to speak to me in private?'

'Yes, my dear mademoiselle. That is precisely what I mean.'

'I believe refreshments have been left in the library,' Diane said. 'Will you follow me?'

The sky had been overcast for days and it was raining heavily. As they entered the library, Diane could hear the steady flow of water trickling from the eaves and dripping against the shuttered windows. She shivered as the dankness clutched at her thin muslin dress. The library was almost chilly enough to warrant lighting a fire and it was difficult to remember it was only the first week of September.

Mr Baker seemed unaware of the cold. He politely refused her offer of wine and, for once, came straight to the point. 'What plans have you made for your future, mademoiselle? I trust you intend to remain with your friends here in London.'

'I haven't yet made definite plans,' she replied steadily, not allowing herself to show resentment at his personal question. 'The Comte was taken ill less than a week ago. He died . . . he died only yesterday. There has not been much time, Mr Baker, to consider my future.'

He did not make the fussy apology she had expected. In fact, Diane reflected, the man she saw in front of her today seemed subtly altered from the obsequious lawyer she had known all of her adult life. She watched as he placed the tips of his fingers delicately together and examined them with apparent fascination. For some inexplicable reason, she shuddered.

'You don't wish to visit Paris?' he asked. 'After all, you are a member of the French aristocracy, and the Bourbon monarchy is now safely restored.'

'I should like to see Paris some day,' Diane said. 'But I've lived all my life in England, Mr Baker, and I imagine my future, too, will lie here.'

'Perhaps it will, although that was not what your father planned for you.' With seeming irrelevance he added, 'Did you know, mademoiselle, that I was born in France?'

'You are an émigré? No, I never knew, Mr Baker. Was your father a lawyer before the Revolution?'

A faint flicker of emotion distorted the lawyer's normally bland features. 'No, Mademoiselle de Verette. Before the Revolution my father was a baron, living on his estates in Normandy.'

'I'm sorry,' she said simply. 'So many people lost so much. It will be a relief for everyone, French and English alike, to know that the endless years of war are finally behind us.'

'I'm not sure that I share your faith in the peace-keeping powers of King Louis XVIII. His conduct

since regaining his throne has not been such as to
inspire even the most optimistic of us with con-
fidence. The Bourbons, I fear, are painfully slow
learners. But now, Mademoiselle de Verette,
let us turn to happier topics. You will be pleased
to know that you can face the future without
financial worries of any sort. You are, my dear
mademoiselle, the possessor of a comfortable
fortune.'

'Yes. I have always known my father was luckier
than most émigrés. He escaped from France before
the Terror was at its height and managed to bring
most of the family jewels with him to England.'

'Ah yes . . . the jewels. The Verette jewels,
however, were merely the foundation of your
father's fortune. I have always described myself as
your father's man of affairs, but the term is not
strictly accurate. We were partners, mademoiselle.
Together he and I have built a most lucrative trade
with the Americas. Americans, you know, are still
colonials at heart. They are so painfully short of
those little refinements that make life worth living.
They are positively grateful to pay anybody who is
able to ship them some small share in the civilised
comforts of Europe. I have heard that even quite
humble American women will not get married
without the benefit of at least one pair of French
silk stockings.'

'You mean the Comte was involved in *trade*?'
Diane did not attempt to conceal her astonishment.
If Mr Baker had said her father was a murderer, she
could hardly have felt more astonished.

'Actively involved, my dear Mademoiselle de

Verette, both with the United States and with the countries of South America. With all due modesty, I may say we have done very well together. And I am delighted to be able to tell you that so great was the Comte's faith in my good judgment that he has made me your guardian and the trustee of your fortune until you marry. I shall be watching over you from now on, guiding your every step.'

'How . . . wonderful.'

'If you marry with my approval, mademoiselle, control of your fortune immediately passes out of my hands.' Mr Baker abruptly ceased contemplation of his fingertips. 'On the other hand, in the unlikely event of your deciding to marry without my consent, your fortune becomes mine to dispose of as I wish.'

Diane clenched her hands tightly in her lap. 'My father obviously had great faith in your judgment, Mr Baker. And in your benevolence.'

'Yes, you are quite right, my dear. And I am sure you will find me the most accommodating of guardians.' He peered at her through the thick lenses of his spectacles, then smiled with avuncular condescension.

'Well, now that we understand each other so well, I must inform you of your father's plans for your future. I believe you are acquainted with Captain the Honourable William Moreton?'

'Captain Moreton? Yes, the name is familiar. I think we met several times last season, although I can't quite recall where. Perhaps at Almack's?'

'I'm delighted that you remember the young man. You will be interested to know that your father decided shortly before his final illness that you should marry Captain Moreton. I am naturally anxious to see that his wishes are carried out.'

Diane's mouth fell inelegantly open. 'Marry?' she gasped. 'Marry Captain Moreton? But we scarcely know one another!'

'Marriage, my dear mademoiselle, usually lasts for many years. You will have ample opportunity to become better acquainted with your husband after you are wed. If you wish to further the acquaintance, that is.'

'But did Captain Moreton suggest to my father that we should marry? We can't have spoken together more than a half dozen times! Indeed, aside from the fact that the poor man had lost an eye at Waterloo and laughed a great deal at his own jokes, I remember almost nothing about him. Why does he want to marry me?'

'Captain Moreton doesn't yet know that he wishes to marry you. I rely upon you to convince him by the end of the year. Shall we say by the middle of December? He will be leaving the country before January is over, and you must be wed by then.'

Diane pressed a hand against her forehead, which was suddenly aching fiercely. She drew in a deep breath. 'Mr Baker, I don't understand you.'

'It is quite simple, my dear. Captain Moreton will be leaving for the island of St Helena late in January to take charge of the British garrison there. I wish you to accompany him as his wife. I assure you that the Comte, were he alive, would enthusiastically support my wishes.'

Diane gasped, then spoke slowly, choosing her words with care. 'General Napoleon Buonaparte is being held prisoner on St Helena. I can't imagine any reason to visit the island, except to see Napoleon. I have heard that it's nothing more than a hot, barren pile of rock in the middle of the Atlantic Ocean, miles from anywhere.'

'Over eleven hundred miles from the continent of Africa and four thousand miles from London. That, my dear mademoiselle, is precisely why the English Government has chosen to imprison the Emperor there. They want no more escapes.'

Diane stood up and moved restlessly towards the shuttered windows. She couldn't help shivering although the atmosphere of the room had begun to seem oppressive rather than cold. 'I have no desire to marry Captain Moreton, and even less desire to find myself isolated on a rock in the middle of the Atlantic. And I certainly have no wish to speak to General Buonaparte.' She swung round to face Mr Baker. 'Why do you want me to marry this Captain Moreton, a man I have scarcely met? How do I know that in marrying him I am actually obeying my father's command?'

The lawyer reached inside his black coat and withdrew a letter. 'Your father revised his will only last month, mademoiselle, and at that time he wrote this letter to you. Please study it, and then decide whether or not your father wished you to accept my plans for your future.'

Diane's hand was quite steady when she took the letter, although her heart was pounding so fast she felt breathless. She broke the crested seal and rapidly glanced over the neat black lines of her father's handwriting. She had hoped to read the words of love that had never been expressed during the Comte's lifetime. Instead she read only a precise, unemotional, request for obedience to Mr Baker's wishes. She re-read the final sentence several times. 'I have always admired your intelligence and clarity of vision. I rely upon you not to fail me in this, the most important endeavour we have ever undertaken.'

Diane carefully re-folded the letter. There was no trace of emotion in her voice when she finally spoke. 'Why do you and my father want me to marry Captain Moreton?'

'Because we need somebody on St Helena who is on our side. There are less than eight hundred Europeans on the island and only a handful of them have access to Napoleon's quarters at Longwood. Visitors are carefully screened before they are allowed to speak privately to him. We need somebody who can pass freely between the garrison and the Emperor's home. We have chosen you, mademoiselle, to be our emissary to the Emperor.'

She whirled round from the window, unable to contain her growing fear any longer. 'What do you mean, I am to be your emissary to Napoleon?'

'Come now, my dear mademoiselle. You are your father's daughter and therefore you cannot possibly be a fool. My meaning is clear. Your father and I, together with a small group of other loyal Frenchmen, planned to return the Emperor Napoleon to his rightful place at the head of the

French nation. But first we must free him from St Helena.'

Diane sat down on a chair with a distinct, inelegant thump. 'But my father never supported Napoleon! He called him an upstart, a usurper!'

'Your father recognised fifteen years ago that Napoleon was a genius, the sort of natural leader who comes along less than once in a lifetime. The Comte also realised that his support would be more valuable to Napoleon's cause if it was not openly declared.'

'You mean my father was working for Napoleon's victory? All these years while we lived in London, he was hoping the English would be defeated?' Diane's voice was no more than a thread of sound. 'How was he supporting Napoleon's cause? With money?'

'Occasionally. Our business enterprises flourished because we had personal safe conducts from the Emperor that enabled us to run the French naval blockade. In return, we were happy to provide funds to deserving causes. But your father's major contribution was the gathering of information for the Emperor. The Comte was much admired by London society, mademoiselle. He had access to the innermost circles of the British Government, and the advice he sent to Napoleon helped to make several French victories possible.'

'I see. In brief, Mr Baker, you are telling me that my father was a spy, who used his friendship with his English acquaintances to betray their interests to the enemy.'

For the first time since she had known him,

Diane saw Mr Baker truly angry. 'Your father was a loyal Frenchman, mademoiselle. He served his country to the best of his ability and to the limits of his skill. You are a Frenchwoman. Eight centuries of the most noble French blood runs in your veins. The English are our enemies. They have always been our enemies, and that is why they are so determined to defeat Napoleon. Not because he is a threat to the peace of Europe, or for any other noble reason. They fight him because he is a great Frenchman and the only obstacle to English domination of the commerce of the entire world.'

'It was Napoleon who invaded Italy and Austria and Germany and Russia, and tried also to invade England,' Diane said with deceptive mildness. 'It was not King George who redrew the map of Europe and installed his relatives on every available throne. Even now, when the victory is his, the Prince Regent has expressed no desire to acquire European kingdoms for his brothers to govern. He is quite content to remain an English gentleman, and so are his brothers.'

'You have met the Prince Regent, mademoiselle. You know as well as I do that he long ago stopped thinking about anything save his belly. His planning is limited to making preparations for his next meal. Do not compare such an apology for a prince with the man who conquered half the civilised world.'

'He never conquered England.'

'The English, mademoiselle, were saved by the Russian winter.' Mr Baker's smile contained no warmth and little humour. 'Besides, the game is not yet finally over. Remember, my dear, that your father was counting on you. You have seen the letter he wrote. Everything he ever worked for during his years of exile now rests in your hands.'

Diane felt the blood drain from her cheeks, and it was some time before she spoke again. 'Mr Baker, even if I agreed to help you, what you ask is impossible. How could I outwit an entire British garrison? More to the point, how am I ever to persuade Captain Moreton to marry me? I have already told you that we scarcely know one another. What makes you suppose that I have only to decide to marry a man in order to accomplish my objective? It is absurd, if you will forgive me speaking plainly, to announce that by December of this year I am to secure Captain Moreton's affections. How in the world am I to achieve such a thing?'

'In any other woman, my dear Mademoiselle de Verette, I would consider your question no more than a request for a compliment. You must be aware of your quite remarkable physical attributes.'

'I have two eyes, a nose and a mouth,' she replied angrily. 'I am of average height and possess all my teeth. I am fortunate enough to be blessed with a clear complexion. The same could be said of many of the young girls in London.'

'Indeed it could. But I will remind you once again that you are not a fool, mademoiselle. You must know that your particular combination of black hair, green eyes and flawless skin is quite—spectacular. You have been the rage of London society for the past two seasons.'

Mr Baker returned to a study of his fingernails. 'Of course, I will not deny that the attractions of your fortune must be considerable to any man, particularly to a younger son such as Captain Moreton. I see no reason at all why you should not attract his interest. And once you have engaged his attention, I rely upon you to see that a proposal follows in swift order.'

'But Mr Baker, this whole scheme is impossible! Where am I to meet Captain Moreton? I can't bang on his front door and offer myself up for his inspection.'

'I am well aware of the hypocrisy of English social convention.' Mr Baker's voice was cold. 'I know that marriages here are arranged with exactly the same practical goals as they are in France. I also know that, in London, it is necessary to dress up these practical arrangements in a romantic froth that conceals their true nature. Don't worry. We shall devise a love story that will have all the hearts of London a-flutter.'

'I trust London society is as easy to deceive as you believe.'

'You have spent two seasons moving amidst the so-called cream of English society. How can you have any doubts?'

'I'm afraid you have an exaggerated idea of my powers of persuasion, Mr Baker.'

'Not at all. I merely repeat your father's views. You forget that I shared the Comte's confidences, my dear. I am aware of how many proposals of marriage you have received these past two years— and that you have turned every one of them down.'

'Oh yes!' Her brittle laugh contained a hint of hysteria. 'You see, Mr Baker, I was waiting to make a love match.'

He smiled thinly. 'Your father is dead, and it is time for you to put such childish fantasies behind you. Only peasants can afford the luxury of marrying for love. I shall repeat one final time that the Comte was relying on you, his only child, to carry out his most cherished plans. Do not fail him, I beg.'

Diane walked to the empty fireplace and stared blindly at the painted firescreen. Her heart began to pound with a rapid, erratic rhythm and she knew she was taking a decision that would affect the entire course of her life. She smoothed her father's letter with nervous fingers and glanced abstractedly around the room. She thought how amazing it was that nothing in there seemed changed. Even the windows framed the same grey scene, for the rain still fell with gentle but unremitting persistence.

It was several minutes before she looked up and met the lawyer's gaze. But, in the end, she spoke without faltering. 'What must I do, Mr Baker, to bring myself to Captain Moreton's attention?'

The faintest relaxation of his posture was the only visible sign of Mr Baker's relief, and his words made no overt acknowledgment of Diane's commitment to the cause of the Emperor's freedom. His voice, however, contained a faint new thread of excitement.

'By a stroke of great good fortune, the Captain's father died two months ago and the family is still officially in mourning. His absence from town gives us a couple of weeks to make our plans, secure in the knowledge that he cannot be forming any other attachment. Our first task is to find you a chaperon of impeccable credentials. Our second and more difficult task is to devise some story to explain why your own period of mourning for the Comte has been cut so short.'

She bit her lip, determined not to utter any protest about lack of respect to her father's memory. After all, if she could trap a man into marriage under false pretences and plan to set free an Emperor, it seemed a mere trifle to worry about mere social convention. She clasped her arms tightly around her body, and found to her surprise that she was shaking.

'When we have invented the necessary lies, Mr Baker, how do I re-introduce myself to Captain Moreton?'

'I have friends to help us, mademoiselle. A party will be arranged. You and the Captain will sit next to each other at dinner. From there, the matter will be entirely in your own capable hands.'

'I may not succeed.'

'Of all the British officials journeying to St Helena, we have chosen Captain Moreton precisely because we are confident that you will have no difficulty in convincing him that he wishes to marry you.'

The trembling of her body refused to stop. 'When I meet Napoleon, if I do eventually meet him, what shall I say? How will he know that he can trust me? How can I organise an escape route for a man guarded by an entire naval fleet and a regiment of soldiers?'

'One step at a time, mademoiselle. For the time being, you must concentrate on becoming betrothed to Captain Moreton. When your ship is leaving for St Helena, you will be told the next stage of our plan.'

The enormity of what she was doing struck her with sudden sharp force. The lives of thousands of people might be affected by the decisions she took today. Panic overwhelmed her. 'Mr Baker, I don't think I can do this! We have peace in Europe at last after twenty years of war. It's not right . . . Even for my father's sake, I am not capable of betraying my country . . . of deceiving the man I marry.'

Mr Baker rose to his feet in a leisurely manner. 'Mademoiselle de Verette, an unjust peace never endures. Even if we did nothing, Louis XVIII's perch on his throne would never be secure. Think only that you are working in the service of a noble cause and that the destiny of France may rest upon your—exquisite—shoulders. Remember that you are your father's daughter. Remember that his blessing goes with you, and all else will seem easy.'

Diane said nothing, and the lawyer bowed low over her hand. 'I shall take my leave,' he said ponderously and, as he spoke, he seemed to shrink back again into the familiar, humble figure she had known for years. 'I shall, of course, see you at the services for your beloved Papa.'

'Yes. Goodbye, Mr Baker.'

'I would rather say *au revoir*. Perhaps you will allow me to suggest the name of a suitable

chaperon? I shall call early next week.' The lawyer
paused with his hand on the porcelain handle of the
library door. 'You will find Captain Moreton an
amiable young man, blessed with a fast sword-arm
and only a modest supply of brains. His elder
brother, however, is a very different kettle of fish. I
warn you, mademoiselle, to keep an alert eye on
Lord Moreton. The Captain does nothing without his brother's approval, and Lord Moreton's
opposition would be fatal to our plans.'

He slipped quietly through the library door, a
black shadow fading into the darkness of the hall.
Diane waited until the last faint echo of his footsteps had died away before she returned upstairs to
the Comte's bedroom.

The golden cover remained as smooth as ever,
the pale face looked as grim as it had done an hour
earlier. Diane sank on to the chair at the side of the
bed.

'Don't worry, Papa.' The words formed silently
in her head. 'I won't fail you this time. This time
you will really be proud of me. At last.'

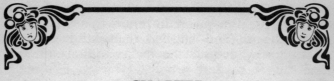

CHAPTER
TWO

CAPTAIN THE Honourable William Moreton did not wait for the servant to announce him. He rushed into the library of his brother's town-house, dropping his hat and cane on to an empty chair and adjusting the black silken patch over his eye with an automatic, unthinking gesture.

'Thank God you've finally reached town, Edward!' he exclaimed. 'I thought you were going to stay buried in the country for ever. Don't you realise that it's nearly the end of December and I shall be leaving the country in three and a half weeks?'

Edward, fifth baron of Moreton and Wellespont, calmly returned his quill to the chased silver inkstand before standing up to greet his brother. The resemblance between the two was marked, although the handsome regularity of Captain Moreton's features was somewhat distorted by the black eye-patch, and Lord Moreton's grey eyes gleamed with a cynicism totally absent from his younger brother's expression.

A faint, affectionate smile touched the corners of Lord Moreton's mouth as he shook his brother's hand. 'Thank you, William, for the warmth of your greeting.' There was no more than a trace of irony in his voice. 'I'm happy to report that I'm in excellent health and had an uneventful journey up to town, despite the icy conditions of the road.'

Captain Moreton had the grace to look somewhat discomfited. 'Dash it all, Edward, I dare say I should have enquired about your journey, but I've been in a devil of a state these past few days. I thought you would never get here!' He drew in a deep breath. 'Tell me, how is Mama? How is Juliana?'

'Our mother is in her usual state of robust health, although she is currently attempting to live on honey and sour milk, a régime which she assures me the Ancient Greeks found amazingly beneficial. Our sister and brother-in-law are both well and bid me give you their love. I am commanded to say that we all missed you at Christmas.'

'I was sorry not to have been at Wellespont, but you know why I had to remain in town. I explained it all to you in my letters.' Captain Moreton paced agitatedly about the room. 'Edward, I have the most urgent business to discuss with you.'

'Yes, I rather gathered that.' Lord Moreton walked with seeming casualness towards the study window, drawing back the green satin draperies to look out into the small, formal garden. He hoped his brother would be too excited to notice the slight rigidity of his shoulders and the frown he couldn't quite manage to conceal.

'I apologise for my delay in coming to town,' he said. 'There were matters connected with the estate that required my attention. I would have come earlier if I could.'

Captain Moreton's expression became wryly sympathetic. 'Father left things in an even worse mess than we had feared, didn't he?'

'Father was interested only in the classical civilisation of Ancient Greece; the problems of running an estate in Suffolk were never of the slightest interest to him. And our mother is almost as fanatical as he was. The only time I can remember seeing her set foot in the kitchen was when she wanted to test a two-thousand-year-old recipe for preserving peaches. We nearly lost the housekeeper and three kitchen-maids after that episode, so I suppose it's fortunate that Mama appears temporarily to have lost interest in the cooking secrets of the Ancient World. I'm thankful to say that she and the housekeeper now merely refuse to speak to each other. With any luck, they may remain in that condition for several years.'

Captain Moreton grinned. 'That must explain the sudden improvement in the food at Wellespont. I thought when I was home in September that the meals tasted remarkably appetising!'

'You don't miss the curdled goat's milk cheese?' Lord Moreton's smile was wry when he finally turned around from his contemplation of the frost-covered garden. 'I only wish the problems of the estate could be as easily cured as the problems in the kitchen. Wellespont is in bad shape, Will, and I have only myself to blame.'

'You've always been cursed with an over-sensitive conscience, Edward, old fellow. You can't possibly be blamed for Papa's obsession with the Greeks and Romans.'

'Of course I can't. But we both know that Father would willingly have turned the running of the estate over to me if I hadn't been preoccupied on pursuing a career in the diplomatic service. I wasn't ready to spend my time worrying about how many pounds of wool our sheep were producing, and how many cottagers needed new thatch on their roofs. I was going to control the destiny of nations! So while I danced the nights away in St Petersburg and Vienna, and imagined myself to be a very fine fellow, our family estate—my inheritance—was being neglected, almost irretrievably.'

The Captain looked shocked. 'Is it really as bad as that, Edward?'

'Yes,' Lord Moreton said curtly. 'It is as bad as that. Over the last couple of years, I believe, the people dependent upon our family were sometimes close to starving. You may as well know the worst of it, Will. The bailiff had been cheating Father for years.'

'Good God! Why didn't you say something when I was home with you in September? You should have told me just how bad things were.'

'There was no point in both of us being worried. Fortunately, our sister was already married before the stealing began, so her jointure was secure. And your own estate, thank heaven, was always separately managed.'

'But there must have been some way in which I could have helped *you*! Why didn't you ask me to come back from London?'

'Your regiment needed you here.' Lord Moreton cuffed his younger brother lightly on the arm, then deliberately changed the subject. 'Besides, I had the impression from your recent letters that you would have been somewhat loath to leave town.'

Captain Moreton blushed a vivid red, suddenly looking not a day older than his twenty-two years. His eyes took on a reverential glow. 'Well, it's true, of course, that I was quite pleased to stay in London.' He sighed wistfully. 'Wait until you see Diane. Truly, Edward, I don't believe there has ever been another woman as angelic as she. She is exquisite! She is the most beautiful woman I have ever seen. She is . . . She is . . .'

'A goddess?' Lord Moreton suggested helpfully.

The Captain looked surprised but pleased. 'Yes, that's it! She's a goddess. Divinely beautiful and divinely good.'

'And no doubt divinely short of worldly goods with which to support herself?' Lord Moreton's tone was very dry. 'After all, angels can't be expected to concern themselves with trivial matters like money. That is always the chore of mortals with no claim to divinity.'

Captain Moreton stiffened angrily. 'You mistake the matter,' he said haughtily. 'If you are implying that Mademoiselle de Verette is out to catch a wealthy husband, you are way off the mark. She has an ample dowry. In fact, she has more money than I would wish. She is so perfect in every way that I have nothing to offer her, not even the comfort of a higher income.'

Lord Moreton concealed a faint start of surprise.

'Is there not a great deal of competition for the hand of such a truly celestial being?' he asked, keeping his voice determinedly light. 'Will, forgive me, but this is not the first time you have fancied yourself deeply in love. Are you quite sure you are not just delighting in the thrill of the chase? Are you certain Mademoiselle de Verette returns your affection?'

'We do not feel affection for each other,' the Captain protested. 'I tell you, Edward, we are in love. Passionately in love.'

'Personally,' said Lord Moreton mildly, 'I have always found love an exhausting emotion. It seems that the more intensely one feels it during the first month, the more rapidly one begins to feel boredom thereafter.'

'If you can speak so, I don't believe you have ever been in love.'

Lord Moreton's expression became quizzical. 'Believe me, Will, you are quite wrong. I have been in love more times than I care to count and I am currently passionately devoted to an altogether ravishing creature. She has a body that is intoxicating, I promise you. A mere glimpse of her lying in bed, her curls spread out against the pillows, is quite sufficient to convince me of my eternal devotion.' He flicked a minute speck of dust from the sleeve of his morning coat. 'Unfortunately, my dear brother, I know that by next month the sight of her body will merely evoke a yawn, and her curls will probably make me sneeze.'

Captain Moreton refused to smile. He avoided his brother's mocking eyes when he spoke again.

'Sometimes, Edward, I feel sorry for you. Oh, you have some of London's most beautiful women at your command. Your mistresses, dancers, and assorted birds of paradise are the envy of every young man about town. But you have never fallen in love with the sort of female one can marry. You only know what it feels like to be attracted to a beautiful face.'

'The face is not necessarily what most appeals to me,' Lord Moreton murmured. Seeing that his brother was determined not to smile, he walked to the fireplace, where he kicked gently at a burning log, sending up a shower of sparks and a sudden blaze of heat. 'Very well, Will,' he said softly. 'I admit I have never fallen in love with a woman I could marry. But you, my dear young brother, have more than made up for my omission. You must have fallen in love with at least twenty eligible females since you received your commission. In your first season, I do believe you pronounced yourself in love on no less than half a dozen occasions.'

'This time it's different.'

'I am forced to point out, Will, that I have heard the same remark at least fifteen times before.'

'I am going to marry Diane de Verette,' said the Captain, and the defiance in his voice made him sound particularly youthful. 'I would prefer to do it with your blessing, Edward, but I am of age and if necessary I will do it without.'

'Have you told her that you are being posted to St Helena?' Lord Moreton asked. 'Does she realise that your home will be a converted merchant's cottage perched on a barren outcrop of rock in the middle of the ocean? Does she realise that the new governor lives in constant fear of an uprising by the natives or a mutiny by the troops?'

'She knows all about my tour of duty on St Helena. I'm sure she will be happy to accompany me.' He thrust his chin upward in a proud gesture of defiance. 'We are in love, and naturally we wish to be together. Nothing else is at all important to us.'

'Naturally.' Lord Moreton once again seemed absorbed in his study of the fire. When he glanced up, his face was slightly flushed from the reflected heat, and his dark eyes contained no trace of their usual cynicism. 'Well, little brother, when am I going to meet this paragon of all the virtues? I trust you will not keep me in suspense for long?'

The Captain approached his brother eagerly. 'You can meet her tonight,' he said. 'She is going to Lady Wendell's party. I'm sure you must have had an invitation.'

'Yes, the card's here somewhere.' Lord Moreton turned away so that his brother could not observe his expression. 'I am surprised that Diane de Verette will be there, however. I was under the impression that her father died less than three months ago.'

'It's true—he did die only recently.' Captain Moreton was unable to avoid sounding a little defensive. 'But she intends no disrespect to her father's memory. The Comte forbade her to have an official period of mourning. He told Diane that too many of his friends and relatives died un-mourned during the Terror and that he wanted no elaborate parade of black lace on his behalf. He said life was for the living, not for the inhabitants of the churchyard.'

'It seems a reasonable philosophy, but I wonder how many of society's matrons are prepared to accept it?'

'Diane attends only small parties and musical evenings, and always with her chaperon in close attendance. Of course, she doesn't dance or go to the theatre or . . . or anything like that.'

'Of course not.'

'Wait until you see her!' The Captain's eyes had recovered their misty, rapturous sheen and he ignored the dryness of his brother's remarks. 'I swear you will fall in love with her yourself, Edward! You won't be able to help it!'

Lord Moreton gave a ghost of a laugh. 'That wouldn't suit either of us very well, I believe! Two brothers in love with the same woman! But I am curious about the prospect of meeting her. I do not believe I have ever spent the evening with a goddess.'

Lady Wendell, a middle-aged widow of stout bosom and ample fortune, was renowned for the quiet elegance of her evening parties, and her reception rooms were already pleasantly crowded when Lord Moreton finally arrived. His thoughts, however, were far from pleasant as he followed the footman upstairs to the main drawing-room. No trace of his inner perturbation showed in his expression. His years in the diplomatic service had trained him well in the art of disguising his feelings.

He had never actually met Mademoiselle de Verette, but he had known her father well and was determined that no child of the Comte would ever marry into the Moreton family. He couldn't imagine why Diane de Verette was setting out to entrap William into marriage, but he was confident that whatever her scheme was, love had little to do with it. Like father, like daughter, Lord Moreton thought with a flash of bitter anger.

His acquaintance with the Comte de Varette stretched back twelve years, to the autumn of 1804. At that time he had just been appointed to a junior position on the Foreign Secretary's staff, and he had met the Comte at a diplomatic dinner party given in honour of the Russian ambassador.

Lord Moreton had been an unsophisticated twenty-one-year-old, but his very naïvety gave him a clarity of vision that the more worldly diplomats lacked. He had immediately sensed that the Comte was taking pains to conceal the true brilliance of his mind. Lord Moreton had wondered why.

This first mild prickle of curiosity gradually increased and, when they continued to meet at parties and receptions, he watched the Comte closely. Before many weeks had passed, he was certain that he was deliberately persuading members of the Government to speak indiscreetly. Within a year, he was convinced that the Comte was systematically gathering intelligence for the benefit of the enemy.

As a young man new to his job, however, he had difficulty in convincing people in authority to accept truths that seemed to him self-evident. The

Foreign Secretary patted him kindly on the shoulder, and asked for proof. This, of course, Lord Moreton didn't possess, and he had no idea how to procure it. Five years later, after exposure to the intrigues of the Russian Imperial court, he might have known how to set about justifying his suspicions. But by then his visits to London were infrequent, no more than short, harried stops en route to Strasbourg or Vienna.

He understood why the world at large was deceived by the quaint, old-fashioned courtesy of the Comte's manner. London society was in the habit of looking only on the surface of things and, on the surface, the Comte's disguise was perfect. He dressed in the stiff satin clothes of a vanished era and told nostalgic tales of the Versailles he had known as a boy. His stories were charming as well as witty, and his appearance graceful, if outmoded. He was a particular favourite with the ladies, but he was almost as popular with many gentlemen whom Lord Moreton thought should have known better. It was universally agreed in Society that the Comte de Verette wasn't at all a bad sort of fellow—particularly considering the fact that he was born a Frenchman and had no idea how to hunt foxes.

Lord Moreton had been frustrated by his failure to indict the Comte, but that frustration had been pushed well to the back of his mind during the busy intervening years. It had been rapidly jolted to the front again three days ago when he received his brother's most recent letter. He finally realised that 'the angel' about whom William had been writing with increasing fervour was, in fact, none other than the daughter of the Comte de Verette. Lord Moreton had posted to London first thing the following morning.

His name was announced in ringing tones by Lady Wendell's major-domo, and he quickly put all thoughts of the past out of his mind. He bowed low over his hostess's hand, murmuring courteous answers to her questions without really hearing them. His diplomatic experience had made him an expert in the art of conducting meaningless conversations and he had become a master at telling the convincing half-truth that conceals a lie.

He glanced covertly around the room while he was answering Lady Wendell's polite enquiries about his family. His brother was nowhere in sight, and Diane de Verette, if she was already present, did not stand out among the two dozen simpering débutantes clustered along the walls.

A slight stir in one of the doorways attracted his attention, and Lady Wendell broke off her enquiries about Vienna to say, 'Oh, there is Mademoiselle de Verette! And with your brother, too.' She tapped Lord Moreton archly with her fan. 'I swear, my lord, they are always together these days. Well, you will want to greet them, I'm sure. Isn't she the loveliest young creature you have ever seen?'

For a moment, he couldn't speak. 'Indeed she is,' he said grimly, when he finally recovered his voice. 'If you will excuse me, Lady Wendell, I would like to have a few words with my brother.'

He bowed, then walked slowly towards them,

watching Mademoiselle de Verette's progress
through the room with grudging admiration. She
could play an audience, he thought angrily, with
the skill of a veteran actress.

Her hand rested lightly on his brother's arm, and
her flashing green eyes sparkled with laughter as
she exchanged little snippets of conversation with
various friends and acquaintances. Occasionally
she would turn to look up at the Captain, obviously
asking his opinion with pretty, flirtatious deference. Her raven-dark hair was piled high on the top
of her head. Two thick, smooth curls fell forward
on to the whiteness of her breast and it seemed to
Lord Moreton that, every time she turned to
acknowledge a greeting, the candlelight would
reveal a new, more lustrous, gleam in the dark
masses of her hair.

Her gown was modestly cut and coloured a soft
lavender, presumably in token deference to her
state of semi-mourning. The simple lines of the
dress, however, did nothing to disguise either the
litheness of her body or the delicate fullness of her
curves. Lord Moreton was an acknowledged connoisseur of women, but he knew he had never
before seen one as exquisite as Diane de Verette.

He had been prepared to despise her. He had
expected to be suspicious of her motives, but he
discovered that he had not adequately imagined
just how violent his reaction against her would be.
He vowed at that moment that she would never
marry his brother, whatever steps he had to take to
prevent it. He watched in silent fury as she flashed
another sweet smile at William, revealing a row of

perfect pearl-white teeth. He clasped his hands tightly behind his back, and imagined them closing with tantalising, mocking tenderness around Mademoiselle de Verette's fragile white throat. He had a sudden shocking vision of his mouth crushed against her lips, bruising their softness, and he pushed the image angrily away. He was thirty-three years old, and too experienced to allow himself to be trapped by a beautiful face or a delectable body.

They finally met somewhere in the middle of the room. William, his face flushed with youthful pride, hailed his brother joyfully.

'Edward, you've turned up at last! We thought you would never get here! Diane has been longing to meet you and I have been dying to introduce you to each other for a month at least. I know you and she are going to be the best of friends!'

Lord Moreton smiled, although he could cheerfully have strangled his young brother. If William had planned to announce his marital intentions to the world, he could not have achieved his purpose better. After such a speech in such a public place, the world could justifiably expect the betrothal announcement to follow within days.

'Mademoiselle de Verette,' he said coolly, taking her hand into a brief, firm handshake. 'I knew your father well, and I offer you my sympathy in your great loss.'

'Thank you, my lord. I miss him a great deal.'

'That is hardly surprising, mademoiselle. I believe it is scarcely three months since he died.'

The faintest trace of colour flared up in her cheeks, but she was too clever to pretend to misunderstand him. 'Perhaps Captain Moreton has not told you, my lord. My father specifically asked that I should not mark his death with a conventional period of mourning.'

Her voice was soft, with a tiny trace of huskiness throbbing beneath the words and, as she spoke, the Captain looked at her with an expression of mingled adoration and longing. By exerting an extraordinary amount of will-power, Lord Moreton managed to resist the urge to give his brother a sharp kick in the seat of his pantaloons.

'We must find somewhere we can talk privately,' the Captain said. 'There is . . . that is, we . . . I . . . have something very important to say to you, Edward.'

Lord Moreton's expression remained polite and faintly amused. 'How very dramatic you sound, Will. I have not seen you look so fiercely deter- mined since you asked me to approach Papa about an increase in your allowance. I think you were about ten years old at the time.'

Captain Moreton refused to be diverted. 'Dash it all, Edward, this is not the time for reminiscences! We must talk privately, and soon.' He allowed his voice to fall to a dramatic whisper. 'Mademoiselle de Verette has just agreed to marry me.'

Lord Moreton's heart lurched with sickening force, although he knew he ought not to be sur- prised. It required some effort to keep his tolerant smile firmly in place as he grasped his brother's outstretched hand. 'Indeed we must talk,' he agreed in a low voice. 'But I have only just arrived at Lady Wendell's, and can hardly take my leave again immediately.' He saw how many interested eyes were observing their group, and he deliberately raised his voice. 'I have absolutely no intention of talking to you now, Will. You have just introduced me to the divine Mademoiselle de Verette and it is inhuman of you to whisk me away before I have had a chance to impress her with my charms. Is he not behaving unreasonably, mademoiselle?'

Her smile was almost irresistible. 'I believe he is. I have heard so much about you, my lord, that I am looking forward to finding out if the reality lives up to your reputation!' Her eyes twinkled with a hint of mischief before she turned and laid a consoling hand lightly on the Captain's sleeve. She gave him a quick, almost imperceptible, squeeze of reassurance. 'Lord Moreton is right, William,' she said softly. 'We need to know one another a little better, your brother and I.'

In other circumstances, Lord Moreton would have admired her skilful handling of a sulky lover. As it was, however, he was in no mood to appreciate Diane de Verette's expert feminine wiles.

'Come and see me tomorrow morning,' he said curtly to his brother. He held out his arm. 'Would you be good enough, mademoiselle, to accompany me in search of something cool to drink? These rooms are very warm.'

'Thank you, my lord, I should like that.' The husky throb of her voice seemed a little more pronounced as she spoke, and she smiled up at Lord Moreton in a perfect imitation of shy pleasure. Her eyes, he noticed irrelevantly, seemed to have changed colour and were now an extraordinary shade of blue-green. Like the Aegean Sea at dawn, he reflected. He blinked, amazed at the trend of his own thoughts, and his mouth tightened into a grim line when he saw that his brother was still staring at Diane de Verette with an idiotic expression of devotion. He spoke more sharply than he had intended.

'I will see you later, Will. This way, Mademoiselle de Verette.'

He said nothing more until they reached the dining salon, where he quickly procured two glasses of lemonade and found a small table where he could talk to her with some degree of privacy.

She thanked him prettily, then sipped at the cool drink, pushing one of her lustrous black ringlets out of the way with apparent impatience. It immediately fell forward again, drawing attention to the enticing swell of her breasts as it nestled against her throat and curved provocatively against the neckline of her dress.

His eyes narrowed in cynical appreciation. He wondered how many hours it required in front of her mirror to achieve just that erotic impression of seeming artlessness. He had known too many beautiful women to be deceived into thinking that Diane de Verette could be unaware of her physical attractions. He continued to watch her closely as she drank, making no attempt to break the lengthening silence.

She looked up at last, giving him another one of her sweet, shy smiles. 'Thank you, my lord, I was very thirsty.'

He was suddenly aware that his hands were clenched tight in an effort to control the burning rush of his anger, and his answering smile contained no hint of friendliness. No wonder poor Will was entranced, he thought harshly. She must have spent years perfecting that particular smile with its dazzling combination of warmth and modesty. His anger was suddenly too great to allow him to behave wisely.

'Why have you decided to marry my brother?' he asked curtly.

Startled colour rushed into her cheeks, making her look even more delightfully innocent than before. 'Captain Moreton has told me that he . . . that he loves me,' she murmured. 'I . . . I hope our marriage will have your blessing?'

'You have not answered my question, mademoiselle. I did not ask whether my brother wanted to marry you. I asked why *you* had decided to marry my brother.'

She lowered her eyes so that he could no longer read the expression in them, but her voice was stiff when she replied, 'Captain Moreton is a kind, good man. He loves me, and of course I am . . . I am very fond of him.'

'Of course.' He didn't bother to disguise the irony of his reply.

She looked at him, and he could have sworn he read a touch of panic in the depths of her gaze. 'What other reason could there possibly be for our betrothal, my lord?'

'I have already asked *you* that question, mademoiselle, and I am still waiting for your

answer. In fact, I await it with considerable
interest.'

This time she did not look at him. 'The impli-
cation of your question is unbearably insulting, my
lord, not only to me but also to your brother.'

He shrugged. 'My brother, Mademoiselle de
Verette, leaves for an island in the middle of the
Atlantic Ocean before the end of January. His
departure date does not leave me much time for
tactfulness and diplomacy.'

'If we love each other . . .'

'Even if your love appears to rival that of Romeo
and Juliet, for both your sakes I urge you to wait
before committing yourselves to marriage.'

'Captain Moreton loves me and we want to
marry. Why is it wrong for me to agree to
accompany him on a lonely, miserable tour of
duty?'

He was surprised to sense a note of anguish
underlying her question, but when he looked at her
he could see no trace of it in her face, and he
decided he must have been mistaken.

'Love,' he said harshly, 'is an unreliable emotion
on which to base a marriage. My brother has always
been absurdly generous in the bestowal of his
heart, and I feel it is my duty to warn you that, in the
usual course of events, William falls out of love
almost as fast as he falls in. It would be in-
convenient—to say the least of it—if you found
yourself perched on an overheated rock, four
thousand miles from London, when my brother
decided he was no longer in love with you.'

He saw her draw in a quick, sharp breath; then

she turned away, and all he could see was the shadow of her profile and the dark mass of her hair. 'You cannot expect me to agree that your brother will soon discover that he doesn't love me.'

'Become betrothed to him if you must. Don't marry him until his return from St Helena.'

'I cannot bear to wait for two or three years, my lord. Our feelings . . . our feelings for each other are too strong to permit such a separation.'

'I see.' His voice hardened because he knew, with absolute certainty, that she was lying. Whatever she felt for his brother, it was nothing that could be described as love.

'Mademoiselle de Verette, my brother sets sail for the South Atlantic in three weeks, and I'm afraid that leaves me no time to be delicate in my dealings with you. Let me come straight to the point, mademoiselle. Precisely what would it take to convince you that your feelings for my brother have undergone a sudden change, and that you no longer wish to marry him?'

Her hands, which had been playing restlessly with the empty lemonade glass, were suddenly totally still. She looked up at him, tossing the errant curls away from her face. 'I believe I have not understood you, my lord,' she said very quietly.

'On the contrary, mademoiselle, I believe you understand me very well indeed. Whatever else you lack, it is certainly not sharpness of intellect.'

She said nothing at all, and his anger increased. 'Come, mademoiselle, I shall be even more blunt and, in exchange, I ask you to express yourself with equal frankness. I am asking for the second time:

what are your terms for terminating this farcical engagement to my brother?'

She stood up, holding herself very straight, and her eyes flashed with emerald fire. 'Since we are to be frank, my lord, I shall answer you with a crudity that matches your own questions. I intend to marry your brother as soon as the ceremony can be arranged. There is nothing—nothing at all—that you can do to stop me. William, you see, is crazily in love with me, and I intend to make sure he remains that way.'

She swept out of the dining salon, head held high, utterly indifferent to the buzz of fascinated conversation that followed in her wake. And Lord Moreton, inwardly cursing his gross mishandling of the whole situation, was left with no alternative but to walk quietly from the room, smiling with apparent complaisance at every acquaintance who chanced to catch his eye.

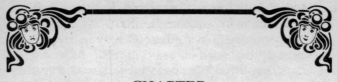

CHAPTER
THREE

DIANE REGRETTED her defiance almost before she
reached the hall; by the time she had returned to
her chaperon's side, she was wondering how she
had ever allowed herself to be provoked into such
an uncharacteristic display of temper.

She slipped into a seat between Mrs Sherwood
and Captain Moreton and pretended to listen to the
orchestra. She schooled her features into an expression of rapt appreciation, then, during the
remainder of the music, silently castigated herself
for her absurd challenge of Lord Moreton.
Mr Baker had told her many times that Lord
Moreton's approval was crucial to the success of
their plans, and she could scarcely have provoked
him more if she had deliberately set out to anger
him. She had no idea why he had managed to ruffle
her so badly. In the three months since her father
died, she had learned to exercise almost supernatu-
ral control over her emotions.

A burst of applause greeted the end of the music,
and she felt Captain Moreton's light touch upon her
arm. She turned to smile at him, aware of a familiar
twinge of guilt as she noted the fervent glow of
admiration in his one good eye.

'How do you like my brother, now that you have had a chance to become acquainted?' he asked. 'He is a great gun, isn't he? Absolutely the very best of brothers.'

'Oh, undoubtedly the very best,' she said.

Captain Moreton, as always, was unaware of the irony in her voice. He launched into an enthusiastic hymn of praise, extolling his brother's expertise in every field of human endeavour. Having touched upon his brother's intelligence, wit, charm, diplomacy, family affection and skilful estate management, he launched into a spirited account of his unparalleled success with the opposite sex, stopping only when the chaperon's discreet cough reminded him that Lord Moreton's virtuoso performance in the royal bedrooms of Europe was scarcely a suitable topic for Diane's maidenly ears.

During the Captain's rhapsody, Diane gradually found her feelings changing from lingering rage at Lord Moreton's arrogance to a vague hopefulness about her own prospects for release from a situation that became more impossible by the moment. If Lord Moreton had even a tenth of the intelligence his younger brother credited him with, he would surely put an immediate stop to this engagement. Any sensible man must realise that Captain Moreton was too immature to form a lasting attachment, and that he should wait to marry until his return from St Helena. The rigours of living for three years on a tiny, isolated island would impose maturity and powers of self-discipline that the Captain currently lacked and which would enable him to make a sensible choice of wife.

Fortunately, a three-year delay in the marriage ceremony wouldn't suit Mr Baker's plans at all. If Diane couldn't get to the island immediately, Mr Baker might be forced to abandon his attempt to rescue Napoleon, and the whole misbegotten scheme would die still-born. Diane would be released from her promise to participate in a rescue plan that went against every instinct she possessed—except loyalty to her father's memory.

Her eyes took on a misty glow of happiness as she contemplated this blissful release from an impossible situation. And all it needed was a little firm-mindedness on the part of Lord Moreton!

She heard the Captain draw in a strangled gulp of air and returned abruptly from her daydreams to the reality of Lady Wendell's music-room. She gave the Captain a radiant smile, wanting to reassure him, even though she didn't quite understand why he was staring at her. He was such a kind, good boy, she thought with a renewed surge of guilt. She would never have agreed to deceive him if she had known how innocently unsuspecting a veteran soldier could be. He had spent two years fighting bravely in some of Europe's bloodiest wars, and yet he seemed to understand almost nothing of the world beyond the battlefield. He had certainly not begun to suspect that life presented a host of problems that couldn't be solved by a fast sword-arm or a swift punch on the jaw.

She looked at him, suddenly wistful, and saw his cheeks flush with a scarlet that rivalled the red of his uniform. 'Oh, Diane! You are . . . you are so beautiful,' he mumbled.

She could think of no suitable response except to pat his arm soothingly. His compliments, for some reason, always aroused her maternal instincts. Unfortunately, her kindly pat didn't seem to have the calming effect she had hoped for and, as she absentmindedly continued patting his arm, some inexplicable force drew her gaze over the Captain's shoulder towards the far corner of the room. Lord Moreton was standing there alone, staring at the pair of them, his face as expressionless as a marble carving, his eyes a dark, impenetrable blue.

Captain Moreton's protestations of undying devotion had never brought so much as a sheen of pink to Diane's cheeks, much less a palpitation to her heart. But his brother's gaze, from across twenty feet of a crowded music salon, caused a strange tremble to start somewhere in the pit of her stomach and rise up her body until her face flamed as hotly as the Captain's had done a few seconds earlier. The sensation was so unlike anything she had ever experienced before that she didn't know how to identify it. She glanced down at her hands without really seeing them, then blinked when she realised that her fingers had clenched so tightly round the Captain's wrist that her knuckles gleamed white. She withdrew her hand hastily.

'I'm sorry,' she murmured, not looking at him. For some reason, she felt incapable of meeting his eyes.

'I understand. I understand completely.' He lowered his voice so that the chaperon couldn't hear. 'Oh, Diane, my *angel*, I can hardly wait for us to be married!'

There was a disturbing new note of ardour in his voice, and she was very glad when Mrs Sherwood chose that moment to announce that she was exhausted and would like to go home before the start of the next piece of music. Diane sprang to her feet with alacrity, never more pleased that her chaperon's contribution to any conversation was invariably to put an end to it.

By the exercise of considerable will-power, she was able to escape from the salon without ever once glancing back towards the dark corner that still sheltered Lord Moreton's silent, compelling presence.

Mrs Sherwood made no effort to converse during the journey home, so Diane had ample time to reflect on the events of the evening. It was strange, she thought, that Lord Moreton had seemed to disapprove of her so strongly, even before he had met her. What could she have done to make him dislike her? She could think of no logical reason. In the last resort, however, his reasons were probably unimportant. All that mattered was that he should put a stop to his brother's engagement before it proceeded any further along its inevitable path to disaster. In three and a half weeks, Captain Moreton would sail for St Helena—and Diane prayed that he would sail alone. In three and a half weeks, with any luck, Lord Moreton would have left her life for ever.

The prospect was not quite as gratifying as it should have been.

Either Lord Moreton's intelligence was considerably less than Diane had hoped for, or Captain Moreton's pleas were more determined than she had reckoned upon. In any event, she soon discovered that her betrothal was considered an established fact by all the parties concerned.

In view of her father's recent death, Lord Moreton and Mr Baker agreed it would be better if the formal announcements waited until after the wedding ceremony, when Captain Moreton and his new bride would be on the high seas and well out of reach of the gossiping tongues of London society. However, with the blessing of Mr Baker and her chaperon—and presumably with Lord Moreton's blessing as well—she spent every evening in the Captain's company, sometimes at a small private party, sometimes in her own home.

Lord Moreton was always present at these meetings, watching her and his brother with an intense scrutiny that Diane found nerve-racking in the extreme. To her surprise, she gradually discerned a faint softening in his manner towards her and eventually, about ten days after their first angry encounter, he drew her into a private conversation, leading her to the far side of the drawing-room, away from the cheerful circle of people gathered around the blazing fire.

He pretended to examine the group of rustic paintings which had been his excuse for leaving the fireside, then turned to her abruptly. 'I owe you an apology, Mademoiselle de Verette,' he said. 'My brother is truly in love with you and I have every reason to believe you return his regard. My opposition at our first meeting was unwarranted and irrational, based upon events in the past that have nothing to do with you personally.'

'Events in the past? Then you have known members of my family previously, my lord? It can only be my father.'

His hesitation was so brief as to be almost unnoticeable. 'I met the Comte de Verette when I was a very young man, mademoiselle, but we were scarcely even acquaintances. If he were alive today, I doubt if he would remember that we were once introduced. I phrased my apology clumsily, and I'm sorry for it. I did not intend to alarm you.'

'Your apology was not at all clumsy, my lord. On the contrary, it was very generous.' She stared at one of the water-colours, which showed five fat and mysteriously sexless cows in a lush meadow. An equally plump milkmaid, whose feminine charms were depicted with an accuracy denied to the cattle, hovered conspicuously in the background.

'I have seen that you make my brother very happy, mademoiselle.'

'I'm . . . I'm glad.' She found it difficult to continue the pretence of normal conversation as she struggled with a sudden, frightening sense of abandonment. She had been counting more heavily than she ought to have done on Lord Moreton's opposition to her marriage, and now she felt the web of Mr Baker's schemes imprisoning her ever more tightly within its sticky strands.

'My brother is almost looking forward to three years on St Helena, knowing that you will be there at his side.'

She searched desperately for some truthful comment to make. She was so heartily sick of lies. 'Captain Moreton is . . . your brother is a most amiable man,' she said at last. A hint of colour tinged her cheeks as she considered the inadequacy of her feelings for the man she was about to marry. The man she would promise before God to love and cherish and obey for the rest of her life. The man she was going to betray almost as soon as the wedding vows were spoken.

The pink of her cheeks darkened hectically at the thought of her imminent betrayal. 'He is very good-natured,' she stuttered, unable to think of another single word to add to her faint praise of the Captain. If Mr Baker were observing her now, she thought dispassionately, he would see how ill-equipped she was for the role he had assigned to her. Telling even the simplest of lies reduced her to virtual incoherence. What would it be like when the destiny of nations hung on her ability to lie convincingly?

Lord Moreton's brows twitched together in faint impatience, then he looked down at her, smiling suddenly with real warmth. He was mistaking her guilt for virginal modesty, she realised. She had forgotten the deadening weight of social convention which prevented any unmarried woman from expressing her true feelings about a member of the opposite sex.

'My brother has found many more enthusiastic ways to describe you,' he said with another warmly teasing smile. '*Angelic* is almost the lowest praise he ever accords you.'

She felt suffocated by the weight of her own guilt. 'I am not in the least angelic, my lord, either in disposition or in any other way. I do hope your brother will not be disappointed to find he has married a perfectly ordinary woman.'

'A woman, certainly. But far from an ordinary one.' Lord Moreton had scarcely finished speaking before he turned sharply away from her, leaning forward for a closer examination of the buxom milkmaid. His face was completely hidden from her view.

It was only a second or two before he turned back from his inspection of the painting. 'I think perhaps we had better rejoin your other guests,' he said, and his voice was once again laced with the mocking undertone Diane had grown to expect. 'I do believe we have stretched our interest in these grossly overfed animals about as far as politeness permits.'

She smiled with fleeting amusement. Even when she was most on edge, she often found herself smiling at remarks Lord Moreton had made. 'I have no idea why the milkmaid is looking so well pleased with herself, have you? Have you noticed that the artist has neglected to provide the poor beasts with any udd . . .'

She stopped almost in mid-breath, embarrassed into total silence. Her unthinking conversation had nearly led her into mentioning a part of the anatomy delicate females never even thought about, much less mentioned in masculine company.

Lord Moreton didn't seem at all shocked. He

merely laughed. 'Indeed, I had noticed that very problem. One wonders how those milk-pails the girl is carrying became so satisfyingly full.'

'I have lived all my life in the centre of town, my lord. I am certainly not going to hazard a guess in the presence of a country gentleman.'

He smiled, then touched her very lightly on the arm, his blue eyes gleaming with new warmth. 'I'm delighted for my brother's sake that he is to have a companion during his stay on St Helena,' he said.

Her breath caught in her throat, and the strange, shivering sensation she had felt once before made her knees feel positively shaky. She was overcome by the overwhelming urge to throw herself on Lord Moreton's mercy and to ask for his assistance in defying Mr Baker. There was no need, she thought, to tell him the whole sordid truth. There was no need to implicate her father or the lawyer. She would simply suggest that she was uncertain of her feelings, not yet ready for marriage.

'Lord Moreton, I need your help,' she said in a low, urgent voice.

All trace of laughter, all trace of mockery, immediately dropped from his manner. 'You are welcome to any help it is within my power to offer, mademoiselle.'

'How very dramatic your offer sounds, my lord.'

Diane whirled round and saw the blandly smiling features of her guardian. She hadn't realised he had left his seat by the fire. She certainly hadn't realised he was so close behind her.

'Things are not always as they sound, Mr Baker.'
Lord Moreton said softly. 'I'm sure you must
appreciate that.'

Mr Baker interposed himself between the two
of them, effectively breaking the subtle bond
she had felt growing between herself and Lord
Moreton.

'Oh, I appreciate it fully,' he said with another
bland smile. 'I imagine that Mademoiselle de
Verette has asked for nothing more than the
support of your arm on her walk back to the
fireplace, or some other equally trivial piece of
assistance.'

'My request didn't seem trivial to me,' Diane
said, forcing herself to meet the lawyer's eyes. He
returned her gaze coldly, making no effort to conceal either his anger or the harsh warning implicit in
his tight, thin-lipped smile.

'I was about to solicit Lord Moreton's opinion of
my father's collection of snuff-boxes,' she said
breathlessly. 'The Captain mentioned to me that
his brother is something of a connoisseur.'

'I see. I, too, have heard of his lordship's fine
collection. However, I fear your interest in your
father's little hobby is making you forgetful of your
manners, my dear. You are neglecting your fiancé,
who wishes to discuss some details of the wedding
ceremony with you. I am the man your father chose
to act as your guardian, and I take the liberty of
reminding you how punctilious the Comte was in
educating you to fulfil *all* your obligations. You will
remember the instructions he wrote to you, almost
on his deathbed. The snuff-box collection can

surely wait to be evaluated until after your marriage. Is that not so, my lord?'

Lord Moreton ignored the lawyer and looked directly at Diane. 'I should be happy to examine your father's collection at any time, mademoiselle. You have only to send word to my secretary, and a time convenient to both of us can be arranged. I understand that you may wish to have the matter settled before you leave for St Helen.' He bowed briefly to Mr Baker and walked briskly back to seat himself on the sofa between his brother and Mrs Sherwood.

By the following Sunday, less than three days remained before the date set for the wedding. Mr Baker called at the de Verette town-house to escort Diane and her chaperon to Morning Service. He brought word with him that all the immediate members of the Moreton family were now in town, eager to meet the Captain's intended bride. Diane, her guardian and her chaperon were invited to a family luncheon with the Moretons immediately after the church service. With the prospect of meeting the Captain's family looming over her, Morning Prayer provided Diane with none of its usual solace. After the service was over, Mrs Sherwood lingered to have a word with the Vicar and, in the crush of worshippers leaving the church, Diane found herself alone with her guardian. When he turned the conversation to the topic of the weather, she cut him off ruthlessly.

'Mr Baker, we have more urgent matters to discuss than the unseasonable warmth of today's sunshine and the possibility of black frost before nightfall. In five days, I am supposed to be setting sail for the South Atlantic. I think it is high time I was given some information about the role I am to play in your plans for the rescue of the Emperor.'

'Be quiet, you foolish child.' His words were scarcely more than a low murmur and his mouth still curved into a smile. Only his eyes, shadowy behind his thick spectacles, gave some faint indication of his anger. 'A public courtyard in front of London's most fashionable church is not the place to discuss such matters.'

'Then what is the place? It seems to me that you don't find anywhere very suitable.'

'That is because you have no need to know anything more than I have told you. You will marry Captain Moreton. If there is anything else you ought to know, you will be informed in adequate time.'

Diane felt an explosion of rage, fiercer than anything she had ever before experienced. 'In three days I am to marry a man whom I have no desire to marry and I still have no idea why I must do it! You have a strange definition of adequate time, Mr Baker!'

He shrugged. 'Captain Moreton is an amiable enough young man. You could find a hundred less desirable husbands among society's bachelors.'

The pent-up frustrations of twelve weeks burst out in moment of wild rage. 'The Captain may be amiable enough, but he has the brains of a pea-hen, and I want to marry him about as much as I want to marry my horse! Why must I be forced into marrying him?'

'Imbecile! Lower your voice!' Mr Baker's mouth tightened into a line of cold anger. 'I will remind you, mademoiselle, that you have already been told exactly *why* you are to marry Captain Moreton. You are marrying him as part of your plan to rescue Napoleon. Now you are merely waiting to find out *how* you will bring our plan to a successful conclusion once your marriage is an accomplished fact.'

He held up his hand to prevent her from interrupting. 'There is nothing further to be said. This subject is closed to further discussion.' He peered short-sightedly around the courtyard until he spotted Captain Moreton's bright military uniform on the far side of the crowded square. 'I suggest that you join your fiancé and his family and that you make yourself as agreeable as you possibly can to his mother and to his sister. You cannot acquire too many allies in the Moreton camp. I am gratified that you have at least had the good sense to get Lord Moreton into your pocket.'

'Mr Baker, please! I cannot carry on this deception without knowing a little more of what is involved!'

'The knowledge that you are obeying your father's dying wish should be sufficient inducement for you to follow any instructions I give you.'

'Mr Baker, I beg you . . .'

There was a tiny pause. 'Your demands are unreasonable, mademoiselle. But I am a generous man, and if information will make you easier in your mind, I shall provide you with as much as it is safe for you to possess. I shall call on you the night before your wedding and give you some indication of how the rescue is to be effected. In the meantime, remember that your chief obligation is to ensure that your marriage to Captain Moreton takes place on schedule.'

'I am well aware of my obligations.'

'Good. Please smile, mademoiselle? You look like a tragedienne preparing for the role of Lady Macbeth rather than a young girl preparing to meet her loved one.'

'The Captain is not my loved one,' she said in a final outburst of bitterness.

'But let us make sure that only you and I are aware of that fact, my dear mademoiselle. Smile, if you please. It is a necessity for a betrothed woman.'

Mr Baker returned his hat to his head with a distinct thump, betraying the fact that he was unusually rattled. He stalked off, leaving Diane staring disconsolately across the courtyard in the direction of her fiancé. For a moment, she rebelled at her lot and turned on her heel, half-thinking that she might return to the church. What would the Vicar do, she wondered, if she cast herself at his feet and pleaded for sanctuary? The absurd thought was almost enough to make her smile.

She found her passage blocked by a solid expanse of masculine chest clothed in white linen and grey superfine. She looked up to meet the disconcertingly penetrating gaze of Lord Moreton's dark blue eyes.

The panic she felt was so acute she could almost taste it. She had been so certain that Lord Moreton was with the rest of his family on the other side of the courtyard—and yet here he was, scarcely two feet away from her. The colour drained from her cheeks as she thought back over her conversation with Mr Baker. Dear heaven, if he had overheard even a small part of what she had said, she was likely to find herself locked up in the Tower!

'You don't appear pleased to see me, Mademoiselle de Verette. In fact, you look quite white. I trust you are not indisposed?'

She told herself that the mockery in his tone was no sharper than it usually was. And surely, if he had heard *anything* of what she had been saying, he would not open the conversation by discussing the state of her complexion? She struggled to force a few words past her lips, which felt as if they had just become permanently paralysed.

'M-my lord, I didn't expect to see you here.'

'Did you not? But I always attend Morning Service on Sundays, mademoiselle.'

'Oh yes, I'm sure you do. I meant only that I thought you were with your family on the other side of the courtyard. I was not aware that you were here, in this precise spot. You gave no indication of your presence when I was talking with Mr Baker.' She realised that she was gabbling, and clamped her lips tightly together. Now that she had started speaking, it seemed to be difficult to stop the terrified rush of words from pouring out.

'Were you talking with Mr Baker? I don't see him here.'

'No. I mean, yes, he was here and I was talking

with him, but he has left me now. He has gone away.'

'But not too far, I trust. We are so much looking forward to enjoying his company at luncheon.'

'Oh, he will be there. I am sure of it.'

Lord Moreton bent solicitiously towards her. 'You really don't look well, mademoiselle. Allow me to offer you my arm across the courtyard. I know you will be longing to meet my mother and my sister, since they are so soon to form part of your own new family. Just think of it! Only three days until you become the Honourable Mrs Moreton. I am quite certain your heart must beat a little faster at the prospect. A love match is a wonderful thing, is it not, mademoiselle?'

'Wonderful,' she whispered. For a few despairing moments she was absolutely certain Lord Moreton was merely toying with her, teasing her like an angry cat waiting to rip her apart at the kill. Then he looked at her with his usual polite, reserved smile and she decided that she was letting her guilty conscience colour her judgment.

She rested her hand reluctantly upon his arm. She had no wish to touch him, but she doubted her ability to walk in a straight line without some form of assistance.

She was only hazily aware of her introduction to the Dowager Baroness of Moreton, and to Sir Alfred and Lady Chester, retaining just enough presence of mind to ensure that she rode back to the Moreton town-house in a carriage with the Captain, his sister and Mrs Sherwood. Relief at escaping both Mr Baker and Lord Moreton restored her to the point where she could behave almost normally by the time they all sat down at the table.

The dishes for the first course had scarcely been laid out when Lord Moreton turned to speak to her. 'I trust you have recovered from your slight indisposition, mademoiselle.'

The Captain was immediately all eager concern. 'Diane, you didn't tell me you had been unwell! Are you sure you are feeling fit enough to take luncheon with us? Do you want me to summon your maid? Perhaps you should lie down?'

She managed a light laugh. 'His lordship exaggerates a very minor indisposition, William. I am in no danger, except that I may smother under the weight of your kind concern for me.'

'You are so frail, such a delicate angel! I cannot wait to cherish you as you deserve to be cherished.'

Her fork stopped in mid-air, and she hurriedly returned it to her plate. She turned to her fiancé, doing her best to smile sweetly. 'William, I assure you that I am disgustingly healthy and need no cherishing whatsoever. I don't believe I have suffered a day's sickness since I recovered from a childhood attack of the measles. And that was at least nine years ago!'

His expression merely became more adoring. 'So delicate, but so brave!'

The Dowager, whose attention had so far been devoted exclusively to examining all the dishes on the table and rejecting most of them, finally fixed her gaze squarely upon Diane. After a lengthy scrutiny, she spoke to her son.

'You never could see half the things that were right in front of your nose, William,' she said. 'That's what makes you such a marvellous soldier. If you marry Mademoiselle de Verette, the pair of you will have five babies in the nursery by the time you've been married five years, just mark my words. Look at Juliana.'

All eyes at the table immediately turned towards Lady Chester, who simply laughed and said, 'My mother, mademoiselle, is an avid student of the Classics and has come to consider herself something of an oracle. Her pronouncements, however, rival the priestess at Delphi for obscurity. I believe Mama is merely suggesting that you and I have a similarly healthy appearance. Sir Alfred and I are the proud parents of two sets of twins and, although she will never admit it, Mama is an utterly doting grandmother.'

The Dowager sniffed. 'Somebody has to see that your offspring are given some vestige of civilised knowledge, some tiny awareness of their cultural heritage. I know I cannot rely upon you to do it.'

Lord Moreton smiled. 'My dear Mama, if I recall correctly, Juliana's elder twins are not yet four. Their characters will surely not be irreparably damaged if their introduction to Thucydides' *History of the Peloponnesian Wars* is delayed for another year or so.'

'Who knows what constant exposure to a barbaric household will do to a young mind? Juliana wastes her time with them romping in the snow and playing jackstraws. It is no wonder I feel obliged to take my duties as a grandmother very seriously.'

Sir Alfred laughed. 'Come, come, Lady Moreton, you are not usually so reticent. Juliana stands condemned, but why am I suddenly excluded from your list of denunciations?'

'You ride well,' said the Dowager, as if this was all that needed to be said. 'A gentleman needs to know how to ride.'

Sir Alfred smiled as he turned towards Diane. 'Take heart, Mademoiselle de Verette. Juliana and I have been married for six years, and Lady Moreton has just awarded me my first compliment. Persevere, my dear young lady, and I have no doubt that you will win her approval in less than half the time it has taken me.'

'I could not hope to outshine you, Sir Alfred. I am more modest in my expectations, I promise you!'

The Dowager smiled placidly. 'You don't have to wait any time at all, mademoiselle. I have a compliment to give you already. You are without doubt the most beautiful young woman I've seen in years.'

Captain Moreton beamed with proprietary pride. 'I knew you would be delighted with Diane, Mama. Now you can see for yourself why I am so longing to marry her.'

The Dowager paused in her consumption of a dish of unsweetened milk curds. 'Oh yes, William. I'm not a bit surprised that you are wild to marry her.'

Diane felt sure there was more than a hint of

double-meaning in the Dowager's remark, but the Captain appeared unperturbed and conversation continued to flow easily around the table. The Moretons cheerfully ignored the social rule which stipulated that people should talk only to the guests seated on either side of them, and Diane found herself wishing that the Moreton family could have been a little less friendly. It was bad enough that she should marry the Captain when he obviously needed and deserved quite a different kind of woman for his wife. It was almost worse that she should be forced into deceiving so many other members of a loving, close-knit family.

She felt Mr Baker's short-sighted gaze resting upon her, and she managed to conceal an unexpected surge of resentment. The lawyer was her guardian and he had the power to force her into marrying Captain Moreton, but she suddenly realised that he had no means of forcing her to betray the country she had come to consider her own. She would marry the Captain and accompany him to St Helena, but she would take no part in any plans to rescue Napoleon. Mr Baker was soon going to discover that his powers of coercion did not extend as long or as far as he anticipated.

She looked up and happened to meet the Captain's soft, adoring gaze. She smiled tenderly at him, resolving silently that, although she would never be able to love him, she would make up for that lack of love by being the best possible wife to him in every other way. She would devote her life to making the Captain happy.

She wondered why pleasing such an agreeable

young man should seem such a Herculean task, and why making such a noble resolution should leave her feeling so utterly miserable.

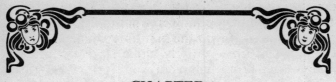

CHAPTER
FOUR

WHEN THE time came to depart, Lord Moreton insisted on escorting Diane and Mrs Sherwood home, politely overruling all protests that such courtesy was unnecessary.

Diane bade a genuinely fond farewell to the Dowager and her prospective sister-in-law, responding eagerly when Juliana suggested that they spend a day shopping together. She shook hands warmly with Sir Alfred, and felt a faint pang of envy when she saw the affectionate glances he cast towards his wife as he admonished her not to spend too much money on useless fripperies.

'Try to dissuade my wife from the acquisition of any more dyed purple ostrich feathers, mademoiselle. I find that for some reason they exert a fatal fascination upon her senses. We already possess a collection of some five dozen that she assures me will be of tremendous use some time soon. I can only pray she is mistaken. I scarcely dare to contemplate a future in which purple ostrich feathers play a significant part.'

Diane laughed. 'I shall do my best, Sir Alfred. But I make you no firm promises.'

With exquisite tact, the family drifted out of the

drawing-room, taking Mrs Sherwood with them.
The huge double doors were, naturally, left wide
open. Even so, it was the first time Diane and the
Captain had been entirely alone since the afternoon he had proposed to her.

The Captain raised her hand to his lips and
pressed a burning kiss against her fingertips. 'I wish
that I didn't have to report to my colonel this
afternoon. I am almost envious of my brother,
since he is to enjoy another hour of your company.'

She gently withdrew her hand from his clasp.
'We have a lifetime ahead of us, William,' she said.
'There will be many hours on St Helena that we can
spend together. In fact, I expect you will soon be
wondering how you can tolerate another evening
with only my face to stare at across the dinner-
table!'

'Never!' he breathed, seizing both her hands in a
fervent clasp. 'Oh Diane, I can hardly believe that
next Saturday you will become my wife. *Dearest*
Diane.'

'The carriage is waiting for us, mademoiselle.'
Lord Moreton's voice cut with unexpected harshness into their tête-à-tête. 'In this cold weather it
would be better not to keep the horses standing.'

'I'll come at once. Goodbye, William.'

A servant waited in the hall with her pelisse and
fur muff. She wrapped a soft white fur scarf around
her neck, forcing herself to smile as she acknowledged the taciturn presence of her chaperon. Other
than her father, she had never known anybody as
utterly emotionless as Mrs Sherwood, who was a
distant cousin of the Count. She stepped into the

carriage, wondering fleetingly if coldness and lack of feeling ran in the de Verette family's blood. Certainly her own feelings for the Captain were unnaturally tepid. Surely any normal woman would respond to such passionate displays of devotion?

'The snow that you prophesied at luncheon seems to be arriving, Mrs Sherwood,' she said, as Lord Moreton pulled on the leather strap to indicate that the coachman should drive off. 'The sky is heavy with it towards the north.'

The chaperon acknowledged the conversational gambit, and for the first half of the short ride they maintained a brisk discussion of winter weather, past and present. Mrs Sherwood so far unbent under Lord Moreton's expert handling as to speak eloquently of her childhood experiences skating on the frozen ponds of her family's estate near Chamonix. Each year, she explained, the grooms had taken her and her brother to explore the icy caverns at the foot of Mont Blanc, carving tiny tables and pristine white chairs out of the solid, snow-covered ice. Her dark eyes sparkled at the memory.

'Is your brother in England, Mrs Sherwood? I do not remember my father ever mentioning him.' Diane cursed herself for the thoughtlessness of the question almost as soon as she had uttered it. There was only one likely reason for the Count's silence.

'My brother is dead,' Mrs Sherwood replied curtly. After a momentary pause, she added, 'He was four years old when the Revolution spread to our part of France. He had his throat cut by the same footman who carried him on our last picnic into the mountains.'

Diane reached out to touch her chaperon's hand, tentatively offering sympathy, even though she was not at all sure it would be accepted.

'I'm so sorry, Mrs Sherwood,' she said. 'I have heard from other friends of my father that it was always such acts of personal betrayal that caused the most anguish. How did you manage to escape from the murderers?'

'My nurse took pity on me and hid me with her sister's children.' The chaperon's voice was once again drained of all trace of emotion. 'I have been told I was an affectionate child before this all happened, and for that reason the nurse could not bear to see me murdered. Somehow she found a way to inform your father that I had survived the massacre of my family and he bribed smugglers to carry me across the Channel. I shall always be grateful to him for offering me the chance of a new life.'

The carriage jolted to halt, and the door was opened by one of the coachmen. Mrs Sherwood, obviously more upset by her revelations than her rigid demeanour suggested, stepped out and hurried up the steps to the house. Lord Moreton and Diane were left alone.

He put out a hand and prevented her from leaving the coach, pulling her back into the corner furthest away from the waiting servant. 'Mademoiselle,' he said softly, 'I regret that there is no time for me to be tactful in my approach to you. I escorted you home in the hope that we might obtain a few minutes alone. You once requested my help in some personal matter. If there is any way in which I can assist you, I beg you to explain it now, before it is too late. I want to help you, Mademoiselle de Verette. Permit me the honour of being of service to you.'

The gentleness in his voice was almost her undoing, since gentleness was an ingredient singularly lacking in her upbringing. She looked up at him, but the interior of the carriage was too dark to see his expression clearly, and she hesitated on the very brink of renewing her plea for help. If she confessed that she didn't love the Captain, Lord Moreton would certainly agree that she ought not to marry his brother. But she shuddered to think of what Mr Baker might do if her marriage were called off at the last minute.

The idea of confessing the whole truth flitted temptingly into her mind, only to be firmly dismissed. Lord Moreton was an English nobleman whose honour and loyalty to the Crown were unquestionable. The cold fact was that Diane had already conspired to commit a treasonable act, and Lord Moreton would never agree to protect her from the consequences of such an act. The punishment for traitors was death, and if she trusted Lord Moreton with the true facts of her situation she might well find that she had frustrated Mr Baker's schemes at the cost of her own life. That price, she decided wryly, was rather too high.

Diane dropped her gaze to her lap, running her fingers nervously through the silky fur of her muff. In the end, she thought, little as she wanted to embroil Moreton in Mr Baker's treacherous plans, it would be better for everybody if she went through with the marriage. Once she had a few hundred miles of ocean between herself and Mr Baker, she would surely be able to think of some way to ensure that his plot to free Napoleon was foiled.

She realised that she had taken far too long to respond to Lord Moreton's offer of help, and she pulled herself sharply away from the restraint of his arm. She was aware of a curious reluctance to destroy the gentleness she sensed within him, but she knew she had no choice in the matter, so she took refuge from the turmoil of her feelings in an outward display of cool formality.

'Your offer is generous, my lord, but quite unnecessary. As I explained to my guardian, I needed your opinion of my father's snuff-box collection. However, Mr Baker has already found somebody who wishes to purchase it, so I no longer have any need for your expert advice. Nevertheless, I do thank you, my lord, for your offer of assistance.'

He leaned back on the coach seat, moving completely away from her, and a pale ray of late afternoon light revealed the sudden expression of harsh cynicism that settled over his features.

'That is your final word on the matter, Mademoiselle de Verette?'

'Indeed, my lord. I have already wasted far too much of your time on a very trivial matter.'

'I was not entirely convinced that the matter we discussed was trivial, mademoiselle.'

She was frightened by his sudden persistence.

Now that she had finally resolved to go through with her marriage to the Captain, she didn't want any probing of her motives. 'My father's snuff-boxes are exceptionally fine,' she said breathlessly. 'But, in the greater scheme of things, their fate must be considered trivial.'

She could hear the sound of her own rapid heart-beat in the dense silence that followed her words. Lord Moreton moved suddenly towards the door of the carriage. 'So be it, Mademoiselle de Verette. Although I regret that you no longer have any need of my help.'

He nodded coolly in the direction of her house. 'I can see that Mrs Sherwood remains in the hall with your butler. She no doubt anxiously awaits your arrival.'

Diane descended quickly, holding out her gloved hand in a polite gesture of farewell. 'I shall probably not see you again until the day of the wedding ceremony, my lord.'

'Probably not. Until next Wednesday, then, mademoiselle.'

The first snowflakes started to fall, blowing around her in thick, whirling ribbons as she walked up the marble stairs that led to the door. She was shaking by the time she entered the hall. Mrs Sherwood ascribed her charge's shivers to the bitter chill of the January afternoon, and Diane made no attempt to disillusion her.

Diane and Mrs Sherwood had just finished dinner when Mr Baker was shown into the drawing-room on the eve of the Diane's wedding. He refused their offer of tea and, after a scant five minutes of polite conversation, he coughed peremptorily. Mrs Sherwood rose to her feet.

'Please excuse me,' she murmured. 'It will be a long, exciting day for us all tomorrow and I should like to retire. Goodnight, Diane. Goodnight, Mr Baker.'

Diane and the lawyer wished the chaperon goodnight, and Mrs Sherwood walked quietly from the room, closing the door behind her. Mr Baker gave a small sigh of satisfaction and came to sit beside Diane on the sofa. His normally reserved features were flushed with unmistakable triumph.

'Well, my dear mademoiselle, together we have done it! I acknowledge your invaluable help.' He sprang to his feet, apparently unable to contain his enthusiasm.

'Yes, tomorrow is the day! At noon, you become the bride of Captain the Honourable William Moreton and the first stage of our plan will be complete. How splendidly ironic it is to think that the first decisive step in the Emperor's new march to glory will take place in a small London church! With one of England's oldest and most noble families as our ally!'

Diane's hands clenched into a tight ball beneath the folds of her satin gown. 'It is certainly ironic,' she agreed.

For once, Mr Baker seemed insensitive to the nuances of her mood. He gave no sign that he had heard the underlying despair in her response. 'I think it is finally safe to congratulate you, my dear, on the skill with which you have manipulated the

Captain's feelings. I confess that I have been full of admiration for the easy artistry with which you have convinced him he is deeply in love with you. It is no mean feat to keep such a volatile young man in the throes of passion for three long months.'

Diane drew in a deep breath, struggling to conceal her revulsion. If she was to thwart the lawyer's schemes, she needed to know as much as possible about them. 'Mr Baker, after the church service on Sunday, you promised me that you would explain something more of how we are to rescue the Emperor. Tomorrow I shall be married, and yet still I know nothing.'

'That is why I have come here, mademoiselle, in accordance with my promise. You should know by now that I am a man of my word.' He delved into the pocket of his waistcoat and withdrew a small silk-wrapped package. He handed it slowly her.

'Here, mademoiselle, is your father's final and most precious gift to you. It was his greatest treasure and I know you will value it accordingly.'

There was no mistaking the absolute sincerity of the lawyer's words. With trembling fingers, Diane reached out and took the little silk packet. Inside, nestled in another layer of white silk, was an exquisitely fashioned brooch. Topaz, onyx and diamonds had been set in pale gold to form the shape and colours of a bee.

'It is very beautiful,' Diane said.

'It was a gift from the Emperor Napoleon to your father. The bee, you know, is his personal symbol. If you touch that tiny diamond, there at the bee's waist, you will discover a hidden compartment in its sting.'

She pressed the glittering diamond and the brooch clicked open to reveal a strand of dull brown hair.

'It is the Emperor's hair,' Mr Baker said. 'Cut by his own hand.' Diane again heard the note of genuine reverence in the lawyer's voice.

'This brooch is to be your means of identification to His Imperial Highness. The Emperor will recognise his gift to your father and will know you are to be trusted, even though you are married to an English army officer. Naturally you should keep the brooch hidden from curious eyes, because the bee is a well-known symbol of the Imperial cause. Wear the brooch close to your heart, mademoiselle, where it surely belongs.'

She was touched by his sincerity as she had never been by his threats or his demands. She carefully wrapped the bee in its silken folds and returned it to the little bag. 'I shall certainly treasure such a valuable and beautiful gift, Mr Baker. Not only because it was once Napoleon's, but also because it was my father's.'

'Ah, mademoiselle, I knew that you would quickly learn where your true loyalties must lie! Together we will change the face of Europe, you and I. Tomorrow we shall see the start of a glorious future for France and for us all! Soon the Emperor will be free from the ignominy of imprisonment, and the French people will rise up to shake off the bitter memories of their defeat! As soon as the Emperor lands on French soil, the people will flock to his banner and Europe will once again reverberate to the glorious sounds of French armies on the march!'

Diane watched the glow of rapture spread over Mr Baker's normally stolid features, and it seemed as though his body grew several inches taller, almost in front of her gaze. She recognised the light of the true fanatic gleaming in his eyes, and terror twisted her stomach into a tight knot of pain. Her hand shook as she clenched it around the brooch. Fate had not been fair to her, she thought in a brief moment of bitterness. She was only a young woman, totally inexperienced in the demands of the world outside her home. How could she be expected to stand up—alone—against conspirators as experienced and dedicated as her guardian?

'Mr Baker,' she whispered, realising even as she spoke that her attempt at protest was useless. 'Mr Baker, have you really thought about what will happen to the French people if there is another war? Peasants all over Europe are dying in their thousands because of years of agricultural neglect. Seeds do not get planted or fields ploughed when all the young men of a village have been impressed into the army. We cannot be responsible for unleashing another war on people still starving from the effects of the last one. The Emperor was a great man, Mr Baker, but can we not leave him to finish out his days in peaceful obscurity?'

As soon as she had finished speaking, she knew that her plea had been much worse than useless: it had been dangerous. Mr Baker's rapturous smiles froze into a cruel twist of anger.

'Mademoiselle, I had thought all such foolish thinking was long since safely put behind you. I will explain to you one last time that the French people will soon be in open revolt against the Bourbon tyrants. That revolution cannot be averted. As a loyal Frenchman, I believe we need Napoleon to be on hand to save the French people from the consequences of their own violence. We need Napoleon to be present to harness and control the potential power of the revolution. And we need you, mademoiselle, as a courier who will give crucial details of our escape plan to the Emperor.'

'But I have no knowledge of any details! I have no knowledge even of the broad outline of your scheme! And the day after tomorrow, I leave England. How can I tell Napoleon something that I don't know myself?'

'Naturally, you will be given more information.'

'But how? When? By whom? You are not coming with me!'

'You surely did not imagine that you would be sailing off into the mists of the South Atlantic without anybody to watch over your passage, mademoiselle? Naturally, I have friends on board the ship. Colleagues of mine will await your arrival in Lisbon, and at every port where the ship docks. As I'm sure you must have realised, I have colleagues on St Helena, although none of them has free, unsupervised access to the Emperor's quarters at Longwood. That is one of the reasons I need your co-operation.'

Diane sank against the cushioned back of the sofa. Dear heaven, she thought, how incredibly naïve she had been! Marrying the Captain would not be a solution to her problem, it would merely be the beginning of a waking nightmare, with her every movement watched over by unknown conspirators, her every step forced into a path that led inexorably to the escape of Napoleon. Marriage to Captain Moreton would not bring her freedom; it would merely ensure that her guardian's trap closed with maximum tightness round her.

Her shock was so great that she failed to think clearly. She spoke before her conscious mind had fully assessed the fatal consequences of open defiance.

'Mr Baker,' she said. 'I cannot marry Captain Moreton. I cannot go to St Helena. I cannot assist you in the rescue of the Emperor.'

One glance at her guardian's face was sufficient to warn Diane of the extent of her folly. The veneer of the obsequious lawyer, never very thick since the death of her father, was utterly stripped away, revealing the clear outline of a ruthless conspirator and political fanatic. He observed her coldly, his absolute stillness frightening her more profoundly than any violent outburst of temper could have done. His short-sighted gaze travelled slowly up from the brooch clutched in her hands and rested lingeringly on the stark pallor of her face.

'Mademoiselle de Verette,' he said softly. 'You will marry Captain Moreton at noon tomorrow.'

She realised that, in the naïvety of her planning, she could not, at this stage, oppose Mr Baker's schemes by any method other than outright defiance. It was too late for cunning, too late for seeking help from some member of the Moreton family. She knew a brief, sharp pang of regret for the carelessness with which she had turned aside Lord Moreton's offer of assistance.

Although her knees were shaking, she refused to turn away from the cruelty of her guardian's gaze. 'You cannot make me marry the Captain,' she said. 'You can deprive me of my inheritance. You can keep me a prisoner in my own home. But you cannot force me to repeat the wedding vows in front of a minister.'

The cruelty of his gaze shaded into scorn. 'Your intelligence, mademoiselle, is less than I had expected. Even though you are only a woman, you are the Comte's daughter, and I had hoped for great things.'

He walked calmly to the end of the drawing-room and poured himself a measure of brandy from the crystal decanter left on a small table. He then walked to the window, parting the heavy velvet draperies and staring out into the darkness of the night as he continued speaking.

'On the day that I first outlined my plan to you, mademoiselle, I had already taken steps to ensure that I would have your compliance—one way or another. You are aware of my political beliefs. You are aware of my plans for the Emperor's glorious future. The safety of months of planning lies in your hands. You may be very sure, mademoiselle, that in such circumstances I have been at pains to protect my own position. If you attempt to voice any opposition at your wedding ceremony tomorrow, the British authorities will immediately find them-

selves in possession of a very interesting set of
documents. They will, within hours, have incon-
trovertible proof of the sad fact that you and your
late father were continuously engaged in espionage
on behalf of the French. Furthermore, and even
more damning, they will learn that you are actively
working on a plot to assassinate Her Royal Highness, the Princess Charlotte. That buxom young
lady must surely be the most beloved member of
the British royal family, especially now that she is
married to Prince Leopold and likely to produce an
heir to the Throne. I believe I can promise, mademoiselle, that if you refuse to marry the Captain,
you will find yourself barred behind the stone walls
of the Tower before nightfall. The chances of your
celebrating another birthday would not be great.
Do you not think, Mademoiselle de Verette, that
you are too young to die?'

The fear she had felt earlier grew until it was a
sickness, invading all of her limbs. Her fear was not
only of the British Government, but also of Mr
Baker himself. Too late, she realised that he would
kill her with no greater burden to his conscience
than most people experienced in drowning an
unwanted kitten.

She feared she had no means, now, to recoup her
mistake, but she did the best she could under the
circumstances. She turned, forcing herself to meet
her guardian's eyes. She pressed her hand to her
forehead in a fluttery gesture of agitation, and tried
to look like a young maiden overwhelmed by the
approaching obligations of matrimony. If she could
appear harmless enough, perhaps—despite her

stupid outburst of rebellion—he would leave her alone for a few precious hours.

'La, Mr Baker, I suppose I must apologise for my sudden attack of bridal nerves.' She gave a little laugh and pretended to catch her breath on a note of girlish anxiety. 'St Helena is so far away from all the excitement of London, I was afraid of being bored. And there are so few civilised people living there that I could not help but think of how lonely I shall be. There will be no parties, no dances, no theatres to attend . . . But I accept that I must do as Papa wished. Of course I will marry Captain Moreton, since that is what my father wanted me to do.'

'I am delighted that you have so quickly changed your mind, mademoiselle. But just to be sure that you do not change it back again equally swiftly, I intend to make some slight modifications to my own plans for the night. I shall sleep here in your house, and then we can both be confident that your newly-recovered common sense will not desert you. It would not suit my plans at all if you suddenly developed a craving to take a midnight stroll.'

Her heart sank as she realised that even her feeble hope of running away and disappearing into the night was being snatched from her, but she forced herself to conceal her despair. True understanding of her guardian's character had arrived a little late, but she finally appreciated exactly how ruthless a man she was opposing, and she would never again make the mistake of attempting open defiance of his wishes.

She gave another trill of laughter, even though

the effort of appearing unconcerned nearly choked her. 'Mr Baker, it is freezing outside, and the snow is thick upon the ground. Why in the world would I leave the comfort of a warm bed to go for a walk?'

'Why indeed? There is no sensible reason that I can think of. Well, mademoiselle, if you will summon a servant, I will give him the necessary instructions to ensure your complete comfort and safety until tomorrow noon, when you will leave here to marry the Captain. Please excuse me while I write a note to my valet, explaining precisely what I require him to do. One of your grooms can deliver the message.'

She swallowed her resentment at his ordering of her servants, and pulled the bell-rope to summon a footman. He arrived promptly and her guardian handed over his note. Mr Baker issued the remainder of his instructions with pompous authority, stripping away any lingering pretence that Diane was in charge of her own movements or her own household.

Mr Baker commanded his valet and three other men servants to come to the de Verette townhouse, bringing with them everything their master would need for the wedding ceremony. Each of the three servants was to spend the night guarding one of the three exits from the house. The de Verette servants were all to be informed that, in no circumstances whatever, was Mademoiselle de Verette to leave the house until it was time to depart for her wedding ceremony. Furthermore, she was not allowed to speak alone with anybody except Mr Baker.

Diane listened with increasing hopelessness to her guardian's orders, her spirits reaching their nadir when she understood precisely how comprehensive his instructions were. If tears would have done any good at all, she could have wept an ocean of them for the folly of her moment of unthinking defiance. As it was, there was nothing to be gained from tears. She could only remain silent and attempt to retain some small shreds of her dignity.

As soon as the footman left to carry out his instructions, Mr Baker poured himself another glass of brandy. 'Go to bed, mademoiselle,' he said, abandoning the final shred of pretence that she was in any way in charge of her own actions. 'It is late, and you have an important day ahead of you tomorrow.'

She rose to her feet, not subjecting herself to the humiliation of useless defiance. 'Goodnight, Mr Baker.'

His voice halted her on the threshold of the drawing-room. 'I shall be sleeping in the bedroom directly across the hall from your own, Mademoiselle de Verette, and I do not plan to close the door. Be warned that I am an exceptionally light sleeper. A mouse scurrying behind the wainscot is quite sufficient to awaken me. And, once I wake up, I regret to confess that my mood is always very black. Do not give me cause to display one of my black moods, mademoiselle. I assure you that you would not like it.'

'I plan to sleep, Mr Baker. I shall not disturb your rest.'

She left the room quickly, before he could say

anything further, but her parting words proved to be, at least partially, a lie. Even after she was curled into the cosy warmth of her bed, sleep remained elusive. Her thoughts chased each other ceaselessly around a treadmill of regret.

If only she had understood her father better. If only she had not longed so desperately to please him. If only she had not agreed to help Mr Baker. If only she had not tried to trap Captain Moreton into marriage. If only she had confided the truth to Lord Moreton when she had had the chance. If only she had not declared her defiance this evening. If only . . .

She finally managed to shut her mind to the endless list of might-have-beens. She had always prided herself on the strong practical streak in her nature, and now, as never before, she knew that she needed to be practical. The past was finished—only the future offered her some hope of change. It occurred to her, as the dawn tinged her room with a soft grey light, that her previous optimism about marrying the Captain had not been entirely unfounded. Whatever Mr Baker's plans, as Diane de Verette she was powerless to stop them. But once she became the Honourable Mrs Moreton, her situation would be vastly improved. Mr Baker might well have spies on board ship and scheming colleagues in every port of call, but she would have a husband who belonged to one of England's most powerful and respected families. She couldn't imagine Lord Moreton allowing his brother's wife to be thrown into the Tower.

A vivid image of Lord Moreton rescuing her

from the dank recesses of a dungeon was the last clear thought to enter her mind before she drifted off into a light, uneasy sleep.

CHAPTER
FIVE

THE WEATHER was bleak when Diane, Mrs Sherwood and Mr Baker set out for All Souls' church, where the wedding ceremony was to take place. The lawyer directed Mrs Sherwood into a hackney carriage, announcing that he wished to discuss some private matters with his charge during their ride to the church. The chaperon accepted his instructions with her usual lack of emotion.

Diane wrapped her pale pink velvet cloak more tightly round her shoulders, and climbed into the coach with her guardian. She had expected no help from Mrs Sherwood, so she would not allow herself to become depressed because none had been forthcoming. She sat proudly, her back ramrod straight against the leather seat, turning indifferently to stare out of the window when the groom slammed the door shut and the carriage rattled into motion.

Clouds covered the sun, and the sky was heavy with a fresh threat of snow, so that the streets appeared gloomy and the interior of the carriage was dark. The lawyer waited until they were scarcely more than a mile from the church before he made any attempt to break the silence.

'It is time, mademoiselle, for you to be told more

about our plans to free the Emperor.' His voice was quiet, scarcely audible above the clatter of the iron carriage-wheels.

'Yes, Mr Baker.' Diane's heart lurched with a volatile mixture of panic and excitement. At last she was going to receive some hint of how Napoleon's rescue would be organised! She had accepted the unwelcome fact that it was already too late to save herself from marriage to Captain Moreton, but, with any luck at all, it wouldn't be too late to frustrate the rest of Mr Baker's schemes.

'It was I who conceived the basic outline of our plan,' the lawyer said. 'Then my friends and I spent three months searching Europe for a man who would enable us to put the plan into practical operation.' He fell abruptly silent, taking off his spectacles and polishing them vigorously on a silk pocket handkerchief. The jerkiness of his movements betrayed the fact that he was nowhere near as calm as he pretended, and Diane froze into immobility. She was afraid that the smallest movement or simplest comment might cause him to cut off his revelations before they had begun.

The lawyer returned his spectacles to his nose and his handkerchief to his pocket. Diane breathed again when he started speaking. 'We have succeeded in finding a trained actor who not only bears an uncanny physical resemblance to Napoleon but is also devoted to the Imperial cause. He is soon to set sail for St Helena in the guise of a Portuguese merchant. He will be embarking on a brigantine in Lisbon, immediately after Captain Moreton's ship has stopped there for re-provisioning. This actor will seek you out in Lisbon and give you any further details of the plan which you may need to know at that time.'

'How can an actor who looks just like Napoleon seek me out?' she asked. 'Will it not be very dangerous for him?'

'You may safely leave all such worries in other hands, mademoiselle. The actor will not approach you direct.'

'But how shall I know when the contact has been made? It will not be easy for any of your friends to approach the wife of a British army officer.'

'On the contrary, there will be no difficulty. The contact will be made and you will know at once when it has occurred.'

She fought to keep her mounting sense of urgency from colouring her voice or even her manner. The information he had so far given her was tantalising, but too slight to be of much use if she was to thwart his schemes. The British Government was scarcely in a position to board every merchant ship leaving Lisbon to search for a man who might look like Napoleon.

'Mr Baker, what if I receive a message and don't realise that it's from your friends? Surely you can give me some more certain method of identifying them?'

'The freedom of the Emperor depends on the wisdom of my planning, mademoiselle. You may rest assured that plans have been prepared to take care of every eventuality. My friends know who you are; they will seek you out. You need to know nothing more except that you should carry the jewelled bee with you at all times, so that you will always have it available to show to anybody who may ask.'

He rubbed the misted pane of the window and peered out into the enveloping greyness. 'We have nearly arrived, mademoiselle, and the icy condition of the road has made us a little late. Please prepare to descend from the carriage. And remember, I beg, what will happen if you should be foolish enough to fail to repeat your vows.'

Mrs Sherwood was just entering the church as Diane got down from the barouche. She turned to greet the lawyer and her charge, addressing them with her invariable courtesy. The greeting over, she walked briskly through the carved oaken doors. She would let the Moreton family know, she said, that the bride had arrived.

The bitter January cold seemed to intensify rather than diminish as Diane entered the small church in the wake of her chaperon. She had little enough reason to look forward to her wedding, and she felt her spirits sink as Mr Baker escorted her through the gloomy portal and into the chilly nave. All Souls' had been built in late Norman times and the heavy grey stone walls soaked up the feeble winter daylight, making the interior seem darker and even more miserable than the cloudy day outside. For some reason, only two branches of candles had been lit, and, although they gleamed brightly on either side of the altar, the rest of the church was left in a shadowy pool of blackness.

Diane repressed the beginnings of a hysterical

impulse to laugh. The overall effect, she thought wildly, was more suited to the celebration of a funeral than a wedding. She peered through the gloom and saw Mrs Sherwood seat herself in the front left-hand pew. Juliana already sat with her husband and the Dowager Lady Moreton in the opposite right-hand pew. The Captain, seeing her enter with Mr Baker, leaned forward and murmured something to his sister before marching towards the vestry. Diane assumed he was going in search of the Vicar. The scarlet glow of his regimentals and the gleam of his white buckskin breeches stood out as he walked away, forming two welcome splashes of colour against the prevailing darkness.

Juliana walked back down the aisle to greet the approaching bridal party. Diane felt her gaze drawn once again towards the pew where the Moretons were seated, and she realised with a rush of despair that Lord Moreton was not in the church. Her sense of loss was so great that it broke through the numbness that had shrouded her feelings during the preceding twelve hours. In a moment of self-revelation, she understood how much she had been counting on Lord Moreton's presence at the wedding ceremony. Somehow, against all reason, she had hoped to find an opportunity to appeal to him for help. But he wasn't here, and now that tiny, irrational hope was gone.

Juliana greeted her future sister-in-law with restrained courtesy, brushing a brief kiss against her cold cheek. Diane had the impression that she gave the formal embrace reluctantly.

'I must apologise to you both,' Juliana said, speaking unnaturally fast. 'My brother, Lord Moreton, is indisposed. He asks me to convey his deepest apologies to you for not being present at this ceremony.'

'I am sorry to hear of Lord Moreton's illness,' Mr Baker said. 'I trust it is not serious?'

'He has a high fever,' Juliana said. 'However, his constitution is strong and the doctor assures us we are not to be worried.'

'That is good news,' Diane managed to say.

Juliana looked away and, in the dim light of the church, Diane had the odd impression that her face turned pale. Before she could ask any further questions, however, Juliana gestured towards the candle-lit altar. 'Look, the Vicar is already waiting with my brother. Are you ready for the ceremony to begin, mademoiselle? Mr Baker?'

'Yes, we are ready,' the lawyer said, and hurried his charge down the last few feet of the aisle, bowing to the Dowager and Sir Alfred as they passed.

The Vicar was a friendly, chubby man, whose bald pate and circle of white hair made him appear more like a medieval friar than a minister of the Church of England. He greeted Diane with a smile, a compliment and a little joke about the wintry weather. She glanced once, nervously, towards her husband-to-be, but the Captain appeared unsmiling and she turned away again, not wanting to meet his eyes. She didn't need any more reminders of the fact that she was betraying a good man.

The Vicar shook hands with Mr Baker, then

immediately launched into a booming recital of the opening prayers. The sonorous resonance of his voice bounced against the stone walls and echoed back into Diane's ears, an inescapable reminder of the wickedness of what she was doing. She closed her eyes, shutting out the unwelcome scene in front of her, and when she opened them again she found her gaze fixed on the Captain's profile.

As tradition demanded, she stood on his left side and the sight of his familiar black eye patch twisted her heart with a little pang of remorse. During the three months of their courtship, she had learned to be indifferent to this reminder of the battles he had fought and the sacrifices he had made on behalf of England. But now the square of silk seemed to assume a fresh significance. The black patch tormented her conscience, a visible sign of the Captain's bravery in the service of his country and a symbol of her own impending treachery.

The Vicar began his recital of the words of the marriage service itself, and Diane's heart pounded with a stifling awareness of guilt. The words of the service dissolved into a blur, then into a muffled roar. She was startled when she felt the Vicar touch her gently on the wrist.

'I shall now ask you and Captain Moreton to repeat your vows, Mademoiselle de Verette,' he said in a low voice. He gave her a reassuring smile, not seeming to expect any reply. He rustled through several pages of his Prayer Book and his rumbling voice took on a more cheerful note as he started reading the familiar questions.

'Wilt thou, William Edward St Aubyn, have this

woman to thy wedded wife, to live together after God's ordinance . . .'

In five minutes she would be married. Diane's knees began to shake, and she knew that she wasn't going to be able to stand upright for much longer. Despising herself for the weakness, she reached out blindly in the direction of her fiancé's arm, leaning against its rock-hard support. As soon as her fingers touched his sleeve, she felt him turn to look at her, and her own gaze was drawn inexorably upward to meet his.

For a second or so she looked at him through a haze of mingled regret and fear. She blinked away the beginnings of a tear, and the haze lifted from her eyes. For the first time she saw clearly the harsh features of the man who stood beside her.

She heard a tiny strangled sound escape from her throat, but the sound seemed to come from a great distance, as though her voice had detached itself from her body. At the same time, the trembling in her legs reached out until even her spine seemed to be shivering.

She blinked, but her eyes still saw the same incredible truth. Despite the scarlet regimentals and slashing black eye-patch, it was not the Captain who stood at her side. It was Lord Moreton.

For a terrifying moment she wondered if she was losing her sanity. Why, in heaven's name, would Lord Moreton impersonate his own brother? She could think of no logical explanation, and the candle flames on the altar began to blur into a solid blaze of golden light. She knew she was only seconds away from fainting when Lord Moreton's arm swept round her waist to support her, its hard pressure forcing her to retain her grip on reality.

He leaned over, smoothing a curl away from her face with apparent solicitude, but the icy expression in his eyes made a mockery of his pretended concern.

'Stand up and say nothing,' he murmured into her ear. His words were so softly spoken that it was amazing they could sound so bitter. 'Repeat your vows when the minister prompts you, or I swear that tonight will only be the first of many you spend in a prison cell.'

Her faintness was swept away in an hysterical desire to laugh. Everybody, it seemed, was determined to see her married. And they were all equally determined to lock her in gaol if she failed to oblige them. She pressed her hands to her head in a gesture of despair, and Lord Moreton gathered her shaking body more closely into his arms, skilfully shielding her from the view of both the Vicar and the small congregation.

'It is too late for any more of your play-acting,' he said softly. 'Repeat your vows if you value your freedom.'

The Vicar appeared at her side and patted her arm. 'Are you quite well, my dear young lady? Are you sure that you are ready for this marriage to take place?'

She managed a smile for the Vicar while she tried frantically to think of what she should do. The minister was obviously a kind man, but could he offer her any practical assistance? More to the point, what practical assistance did she require? Did she want to be rescued from Lord Moreton and returned to the power of her guardian? And would the Vicar agree to help her if he knew the truth? He was a minister of the Established Church, and presumably as loyal an Englishman as could be found anywhere.

'I feel a little faint,' she said finally, hoping to win a few more minutes in which to consider what she should do. In truth, the world still seemed to be tilting around her and it wasn't easy to think.

The Vicar was all concern. 'Shall I delay the ceremony for a while, my dear? Would you care for a cup of water? Perhaps there is even time to prepare some tea?'

Mr Baker sprang to his feet. 'There is no reason for delay, my good sir,' he said loudly. 'My ward is known for her delicate, feminine susceptibilities. But the truth of the matter is that she longs for the marriage to take place *immediately*. Is that not so, my dear mademoiselle? You recall our conversation of only last night? You do not wish for tea, I'm quite certain.'

'No,' she said flatly, 'I don't wish for any tea.' She forced herself to give the Vicar another smile, realising that it would be hopeless to appeal to him.

'I recall our conversation clearly, Mr Baker, and it is as you say. I am—longing—to be married. I apologise for my attack of nerves.'

The Vicar apparently had no difficulty in believing that the pallor of her cheeks and the tremble in her voice were both caused by the delicacy of her feminine constitution. He insisted on giving her some water from the carafe kept in the vestry. When she had taken a few sips and put down the pewter cup, he gave her hand yet another encouraging pat.

'I can see that your husband will have to take great care of you, my dear. But it will be a pleasure to look after such a beautiful and fragile flower of womanhood, is that not so, Captain Moreton?'

Lord Moreton's mouth twisted into a grim smile. 'I intend to give Mademoiselle de Verette all the attention she deserves,' he said. 'You need have no fears, dear sir, that even her slightest moment of frailty will go undetected, since I don't intend to let her out of my sight. She shall have my undivided attention, I promise you.'

The Vicar's benevolent nature was ill-suited to understanding subtle double-meanings. The threat implicit in Lord Moreton's words entirely escaped his notice.

'Young love is a wonderful thing,' he said with a sentimental smile. 'And although you two will find this hard to believe, true love becomes better the longer you are married. My dear wife and I are only just beginning to discover how fond we are of each other.'

His smile stretched into a beam of utter joyfulness. 'The Good Lord has truly provided everything that we mortals could ever need for happiness, if only we would use his gifts wisely.'

The Vicar gave Diane's arm one last reassuring squeeze and resumed his recital of the wedding service. She heard Lord Moreton's low voice promise to love and cherish her, and she wondered why no one protested at the hollow, cynical ring to his words. She forced herself to make the necessary responses, and watched, as though observing the actions of a stranger, when the Vicar took her left hand and joined it to Lord Moreton's.

A quiver of sensation ran up her arm when Lord Moreton slipped an elaborately-chased golden ring on her finger. She stared silently at the ring. She was married. To Lord Moreton. She allowed her hand to drop back to her side, where the golden band was hidden in the soft silk folds of her gown.

The cheerful boom of the Vicar's voice pronounced that Diane Hélène Victoire and William Edward St Aubyn were now man and wife. He suggested that 'Captain Moreton' might care to kiss his bride.

Lord Moreton bent and brushed his lips against Diane's cheek. Although his lips were cool— even cold—she was aware of a strange burning sensation where his mouth had touched her skin. He leaned across to kiss her other cheek, and whispered softly, 'Remember, one word to alert your friend Baker as to who I am, and you will spend the rest of your life regretting it.'

The Vicar ushered the newly-wedded couple into the vestry and invited them to sign their names in his register. Diane was surprised to find that her shaking fingers were able to grip the quill firmly enough to make a legible signature. She saw that her husband had signed his name as William Edward St Aubyn of Moreton and Wellespont. The Vicar, who in any case scarcely glanced

at their signatures, seemed to find this quite
satisfactory. She wondered abstractedly if
Lord Moreton really was called William, although
it seemed odd that two brothers should have the
same name.

Lord Moreton shook the minister's hand in a
brisk gesture of farewell. 'Because of the bad
weather, my bride and I have to leave immediately
for the coast. But my mother and my sister have
ordered a small celebratory dinner to be served at
my . . . that it to say, at my brother's town-house. I
hope you will be able to join them? And perhaps
your good wife also?'

'Certainly, it will be our pleasure. I am only sorry
that you and your beautiful bride won't be with us. I
hope you have some fur rugs inside your travelling
carriage. Your bride still looks pale and chilled, I
fear.'

'Yes, our comfort has been well provided for.'
Lord Moreton turned to Diane with every appearance of solicitude, but she was well aware of the fact
that his eyes never actually met hers without
hardening with scorn. 'Are you ready to leave, my
dear? We should be on our way.'

'Do you not plan to say farewell to your mother
and sister?'

'They will say goodbye to us when we are in our
carriage.'

If the Vicar thought this rather a strange arrangement, he made no comment. He unbarred the
vestry door and allowed Diane and Lord Moreton
to pass through to the road where his lordship's
low-slung travelling carriage already awaited them.

'Why didn't you want us to return to the church?' Diane asked.

She was sure there must be other, more important questions that needed to be asked, but she felt capable of thinking only simple thoughts. The reason why Lord Moreton had decided to marry her still seemed too bizarre to worry about.

For a moment she thought he would not answer even this trivial question, then he raised his shoulders in a slight shrug.

'I don't want your guardian to see me face-to-face. He is short-sighted, and my brother and I look reasonably alike, but there is no point in providing Mr Baker with an opportunity to view me at close quarters.'

'You want my guardian to think I have married Captain Moreton?'

'The answer to that is self-evident, mademoiselle.'

'I am not mademoiselle any longer.' Her breath came out in a tiny gasp of overwrought laughter. 'I am Lady Moreton.'

His expression froze into the iciest of rejections. 'Enjoy your title while you may, *my lady*. It will not be yours for long.'

Whichever way she interpreted this, it didn't sound very promising. 'Wh-what precisely do you mean, my lord?'

There was total indifference in his voice and in his look. 'You will eventually find out.'

He tossed a fur-lined travelling rug in her direction, at the same time rubbing away the steam that had already accumulated on the carriage window.

'My family is leaving the church. Your guardian has been informed that the sailing date of our ship has been moved forward, and that we are in a desperate hurry to start our journey to Plymouth. Keep your goodbyes brief, and do not attempt to enlighten Mr Baker as to what has happened.'

'How could I do that?' she said wearily. 'I have no idea what *has* happened, except that I have been forced to marry a man whom I scarcely know.'

'That situation will soon be rectified, my dear. Before long you will know me intimately—and you will realise that my brother and I share few characteristics, save a love of our country. I certainly share none of his susceptibility to scheming women. I warn you now, madam, that your wiles will not deceive me, however skilfully you play them. I have met Cyprians in the courts of St Petersburg and Vienna who put your efforts at seduction to shame. Don't expect me to call you an angel, however softly you sigh and flutter your eyelashes. My names for you have more to do with hell than heaven. I knew your father, and I have always recognised you for the she-devil that you are.'

She recoiled from the viciousness of his attack but, before she could attempt to defend herself, the wedding guests arrived to say their goodbyes. Lord Moreton leaned back into the far corner of his travelling carriage, at the same time ordering Diane to move in front of the window, thus blocking the view of anybody who might attempt to look inside the chaise. In fact, however, the chill of the January day was so bitter that all the guests were huddled deep into the protective warmth of their cloaks, and Diane suspected that even Mr Baker was paying only cursory attention to the appearance of the bridal couple.

The Dowager offered formal congratulations and a brief farewell. The coldness of her manner was in sharp contrast to her former air of casual friendship, and it soon became clear to Diane that all the members of the Moreton family, including Sir Alfred, were well aware of Lord Moreton's impersonation and were actively working to support it. Juliana's vaguely hostile behaviour prior to the wedding ceremony was now explained. She had been forced to pretend friendship for Diane and had scarcely been able to keep up the pretence.

Sir Alfred reminded everybody that the ship was sailing earlier than planned and, pointing to the snow-heavy sky, urged 'Captain Moreton' to be on his way. Mr Baker, delighted that his plans had thus far progressed so successfully, added his voice to the general chorus urging the newly-weds to depart.

Diane ought to have found a certain ironic amusement in observing the two sets of guests, each intent on deceiving the other, each intent on making sure that she had no chance to confide in any member of the opposing family. Unfortunately, she felt unable to appreciate the joke.

A miserable icy rain began to fall, and the farewells came to a rapid conclusion. The carriage window was ordered to be closed, the coachman sprang up on his box, and the horses were encouraged to pick their way nervously across the slippery cobblestones. Slowly, the iron wheels skating dangerously on the freezing road surface, the carriage rolled towards the River Thames and the start of its journey to Plymouth.

The heavy clouds lifted as they left town, and the road surface cleared sufficiently to allow the horses to maintain a steady trot. The rhythmic swaying of the coach gradually soothed Diane's lacerated nerves, and by the time the horses broke into a slow canter over the frozen mud of the western pike road, her thoughts had finally coalesced into a coherent question.

She turned away from her inspection of the bleak scene outside the window and looked up at Lord Moreton. He had discarded his unnecessary eyepatch, she discovered, and now stared at her with an undisguised mixture of anger and loathing.

His expression did not augur well for the discussion she planned, nevertheless she had to try to make sense of the day's events. She drew in a deep, calming breath, meeting his frowning gaze without flinching.

'Why did you marry me?' she asked.

CHAPTER
SIX

IT SEEMED a long time before Lord Moreton deigned to reply. His gaze flicked contemptuously over her and she wondered how, even in the darkness of All Souls' church, she had ever mistaken him for his brother. Every line of his body breathed an arrogant self-assurance that was entirely lacking from the Captain's boyish figure. Every line of his face betrayed a cynicism equally lacking from the Captain's frank, open features.

He finally spoke. 'I married you for the sake of my country, madam, and in order to rescue my brother from your clutches.'

A frisson of anger pierced the numbness of her emotions. 'Noble aims, my lord, but I must point out that your rescue plan seems badly flawed. I fail to see how your decision to marry me helps England and, although your brother may be saved from my evil clutches, *you* are now hopelessly ensnared.'

His mouth thinned. 'You mistake the matter, madam. My bond to you—distasteful as I find it—will not endure for long. I have the Foreign Secretary's personal assurance that a Bill of Annulment will be rushed through Parliament as soon as my mission is successfully completed. Within a few months it will be as though our marriage had never existed.'

'But a Bill of Annulment will create such a scandal! How can you contemplate such a thing?'

'The matter will be handled with the utmost discretion. The Bill will be passed in a closed session of Parliament and the Prince Regent will sign it in secret.'

'Even if the Bill remains entirely secret, I cannot understand what you hope to achieve by going through such an extraordinary wedding ceremony. Why did you pretend to be your own brother? The events of this whole day make no shred of sense to me.'

'I find that statement hard to believe. You are short of honour, madam, but you are well-equipped with brains. Our journey to Plymouth is sure to be long and tedious, so you will have plenty of time to work out the answers to your own questions. I am confident that you will soon be able to deduce precisely why I chose to impersonate my brother.'

She laughed and, hearing the harshness of the sound, recognised the note of hysteria that lingered in her laughter. 'In truth, my lord, I think I must be a great deal more foolish than either you or my guardian suppose. I can think of no logical reason why you should marry a woman you despise, simply to prevent your brother making the same mistake.'

'Don't try to feign an innocence that we both know to be false.'

'I am feigning nothing, my lord.'

'Does that mean you are finally willing to confess your true reasons for trying to entrap my brother into marriage?'

'Yes,' she said, deciding that the moment had come when she had no choice but to confess the truth and hope for Lord Moreton's understanding. 'I am perfectly willing to explain how I became involved in Mr Baker's plans. But you must believe, my lord, that I never intended to carry out his instructions once I was safely out of his power. I could find no way to avoid marriage to your brother, but I swear I never intended to be anything other than a loyal, dutiful wife to the Captain.'

Lord Moreton's mouth twisted into the most cynical of smiles. 'Oh, well done!' he said softly. 'Such a heart-rending protestation would have been guaranteed to melt the last trace of my brother's resistance. But I would remind you, madam, that I am not my brother. You may spare me the soft blushes and the sparkle of approaching tears. Perhaps it will speed us through the early stages of your confession if I tell you that I know precisely why you set out to seduce my brother into matrimony. You needed an iron-clad excuse for journeying to St Helena because your guardian needed a friend on the island who had access both to the British garrison and to Napoleon's headquarters at Longwood.'

She had realised, of course, that Lord Moreton knew something about her guardian's plans, but she was startled by the extent of his knowledge. 'Is *that* why you married me?' she asked. 'You felt it was necessary to do something so extraordinary simply to stop me going to St Helena?'

'On the contrary, my dear. I married you in order to make absolutely certain that you went there with all possible speed.'

'I don't understand . . . You *want* me to go to St Helena?'

'But of course. The British Government is most anxious to see what you do once you arrive there. I shall take the greatest pleasure in telling them.'

'I see.'

'Do you? I wonder if you understand just how much of your guardian's plotting is already known to the British Government? Several months ago, the Foreign Secretary learned that an active group of Napoleon's supporters, based in London, was headed by the Comte de Verette. Did you know that it was only your father's suicide that prevented his arrest?'

She felt her emotions freeze into a solid lump of pain that seemed to be lodged somewhere tight and uncomfortable beneath her heart. It was almost impossible to breathe, but she managed to make her lips shape a single word. 'Suicide?'

'Your father, so I understand, was in excellent health two days before his death. It is assumed by the Foreign Secretary's office that he swallowed poison rather than endure the capture he suspected was imminent.'

She pushed her hand hard against her mouth, swallowing fiercely until the spasms of sickness passed. Lord Moreton's expression remained utterly pitiless as he watched her struggle for control.

'The British Government is well aware of the fact that Mr Baker has taken over the leadership of this group from the Comte, your father. We know that he and his cronies are hoping to restore Napoleon to the French throne.' Lord Moreton's cool gaze travelled over her with ruthless assessment. 'If you are wise, madam, you will tell me what part you are supposed to play in the ill-fated rescue scheme they are concocting.'

She forced back a final wave of nausea, determined to hide the black despair she felt at the information Lord Moreton had tossed at her so brutally. Suicide. Her father had committed suicide. He had deliberately planned his death and yet had spared no word of love for her, no tiny word of affection or regret for years of coldness. Fiercely she blinked back the hot tears, refusing to give Lord Moreton the satisfaction of breaking down in front of him.

'It seems to me that the British Government knows a great deal more than I do,' she said and the bleakness she felt made her words sound hollow. 'Believe me, my lord, I knew nothing of Mr Baker's plans except that I was to marry Captain Moreton. And I know nothing of what I am supposed to do on St Helena other than wait for instructions.'

The shadows in the interior of the carriage made it difficult to read Lord Moreton's expression, but Diane had the impression that her answer didn't please him.

'Your protestations of innocence are singularly unconvincing, my dear, and they carry little weight with me. You have forgotten that I gave you ample opportunity to confess that you did not want to marry my brother. You turned the opportunity aside, which was certainly not the act of an innocent woman.'

'Surely you can understand that I was frightened!' she exclaimed. 'Mr Baker threatened me with imprisonment! He even threatened my life! I decided that it would be best to pretend to help my guardian until I was safely at sea. Once free of him, I planned to ignore his instructions. I even hoped that, by pretending to go along with his schemes, I might learn enough to make a helpful report to the British authorities.'

Lord Moreton's voice was very soft. 'And just how did my brother fit into this wonderfully noble plan of yours, my lady? You may recall my brother. He is the young man you deliberately dazzled into a state of blind adoration. He is the man misguided enough to worship the ground you walk upon. Did you spare him any thought in all this enterprising planning of yours?'

She bit her lip nervously. 'I have already told you, my lord, that I intended to be the best possible wife to your brother.'

'The best possible wife . . . except for the trivial fact that you do not love him. Except for the fact that you scarcely care whether he lives or dies.'

She felt her fingers twist tightly together inside her muff. 'Your condemnation is unjust, my lord. I have often heard that love grows after marriage rather than before. I hoped the Captain and I might find it so.'

He remained coldly silent, and she looked at him

pleadingly. 'My father had been dead only one day when Mr Baker ordered me to help him. He told me it was my father's express wish that I should marry Captain Moreton. Perhaps it was wrong of me to want to please my father above all other considerations, but I loved him, and it did not seem wrong at the time. Later, when I had wiser thoughts, I was already trapped. Mr Baker would not allow me to renege on my agreement to help him and, in any case, your brother was already attracted to me. Surely you can understand, my lord, that I was a victim of my circumstances rather than a criminal who set out to commit treason?'

'I see only that you are a traitor to the country that has sheltered you from the moment of your birth. I see only that you are a brilliant actress who beguiled my brother into a web of false delight.' He looked at her, his eyes dark with anger. 'I will give you a piece of advice, madam, and I urge you to take it deeply to heart. If you wish to save that pretty neck of yours from the gallows, do *exactly* as I command you. If I am satisfied with your behaviour over the next few weeks, I shall recommend that you be allowed to remain on St Helena as part of the governor's household. If, on the other hand, you are foolish enough to attempt to double-cross me, I shall see to it that you are brought to trial on charges of high treason. You are, I am sure, aware of the punishment for persons convicted of treason.'

'I am aware that traitors in England are hanged, my lord.'

'And I shall personally escort you to the gallows

if you try any tricks. Do I make myself absolutely clear?'

'Crystal clear,' she said wearily. She leaned back, closing her eyes and drawing the thick fur-lined rug more tightly round her shoulders. Her body and mind each seemed to ache with a tiredness that went beyond normal fatigue, leaving her in·a bone-chilling state of exhaustion. She knew that she was beyond attempting any further rational justification of her actions to Lord Moreton, and she tried to relax herself sufficiently to sleep.

The coach hurtled endlessly over the rough roads. Afternoon dimmed into evening, and still they maintained their relentless journey towards Plymouth. They stopped only to change horses and drivers, sometimes completing the changeover so swiftly that there was no time even to walk as far as the inn. By midnight they had covered almost a hundred and twenty miles, a well-nigh miraculous achievement over ice-encrusted winter roads.

Diane's body ached everywhere it was possible for a body to ache, and her head throbbed with a mixture of pain and nausea. She longed to hear Lord Moreton say that they were halting for the night, but he made no such suggestion and some stubborn streak of pride left her incapable of begging for rest. He bought her coffee and hot bread at an inn somewhere in Hampshire, and again somewhere in Dorset. By the time the carriage rolled into the town of Exeter, night had given way to the greyness of another winter morning. Diane stared listlessly towards the inn where they had halted. Lord Moreton sprang out of the coach, ordering her to follow, but she didn't stir. She longed for a cup of fresh hot tea, but she felt too sick, too chilled and too unutterably weary to step down from the chaise. She huddled, shivering, in her corner of the carriage.

She saw Lord Moreton halt in his brisk progress across the courtyard. He spoke without turning to look at her. 'Please don't create unnecessary difficulties, my dear. You need to eat something, and you need to wash your face and hands in hot water. Your muscles must be cramped after so many hours of travel in a cold carriage, and hot water is the only effective way to take off the chill.'

She knew he was right, but she didn't have enough energy to force her aching limbs into action. She tried to get up but, on discovering that her legs wouldn't support her, sank listlessly back on to the hard seat. She retained only one spark of defiant energy: she would pass out before she admitted her weakness in front of Lord Moreton.

'Thank you, but I do not choose to enter the inn. I shall stay here.' Her voice rasped with dryness, but she managed to add, 'I'm not hungry.'

She was bundled roughly into his arms even before she had time to register the fact that he had returned to the carriage. He ignored her croaks of protest and walked swiftly across the rain-wet cobblestones of the yard, carrying her into the heavenly warmth of the inn. He took her into a private parlour and dumped her on the wooden settle which was drawn up in front of the fire.

She leaned back against the cushion that had somehow appeared behind her head and sighed with involuntary pleasure as the warmth of the blazing logs reached out to envelop her. An unwelcome honesty compelled her to acknowledge how glad she was to be inside the inn.

'Thank you, my lord, for carrying me,' she said quietly. 'This warmth is wonderful and I had forgotten cushions could feel so soft.'

He looked at her, tight-lipped, and strode from the room without replying. She felt a curious little twitch of regret as she watched him leave, but she dismissed the feeling, taking off her white kid boots and wriggling her stockinged toes ecstatically in front of the leaping flames. Her stockings soon began to steam with the dampness that had seeped into the carriage and through the thin soles of her boots.

She drowsed contentedly in the heat, and it seemed only moments later that a maid entered, carrying an earthenware bowl of mutton broth and a pitcher of hot water. Diane looked up quickly, but Lord Moreton had not returned with the maid.

By the time she had eaten the piping hot soup and plunged her arms into the water as far as her elbows, she felt like a living human being again instead of a walking corpse. Lord Moreton appeared in the doorway just as she reluctantly finished pulling on her still-damp boots.

They observed each other in tense silence for a second or so, then Lord Moreton made a small impatient exclamation and strode into the parlour, sweeping her back into his arms.

'I can walk, my lord!' she protested. Now that her senses had thawed out a little, she found it extraordinarily disturbing to be carried so close to Lord Moreton's chest.

'We are late,' he said curtly. 'I cannot wait while you teeter across the courtyard.'

He returned her unceremoniously to her corner of the carriage, then seated himself as far away from her as space allowed. As soon as he had given the order to depart, he closed his eyes. To the best of Diane's knowledge, he did not open them again until they arrived in Plymouth, five weary hours later.

This time he did not carry her into the inn. He waited with obvious impatience while she descended from the carriage, barely concealing his irritation when she stumbled and he was forced to reach out to prevent her from falling.

The innkeeper was apparently expecting them. He greeted Lord Moreton by name and cast several interested, though disapproving, glances in Diane's direction. Lord Moreton made no attempt to alleviate the innkeeper's curiosity by introducing her. He simply asked to be shown into their suite of rooms and tossed a handful of silver coins on the wooden counter in order to ensure prompt service. The innkeeper scooped the coins into a purse hanging from his waist, bowed obsequiously, and directed a maidservant to conduct the distinguished visitors to their rooms. The silver effectively answered any questions he might have had about the respectability of his visitors.

Diane barely managed to follow Lord Moreton up the shallow stairs without falling over from weariness. The little maidservant who had led the way pushed open a heavy oaken door and Lord Moreton entered, Diane trailing in his wake. She walked almost blindly in the direction of the fireplace, then came to a dead halt when she realised there was already somebody in the room.

She looked up, feeling a tremor of despair run through her when she recognised the silent figure standing by the chimney-piece, staring broodingly into the glow of the fire. It was Captain Moreton.

The Captain turned and looked at her briefly, with no trace of his former devotion. When he had taken in every detail of her bedraggled appearance, his gaze shifted towards his brother. 'You've made good time, Edward,' he said.

'Yes.' Lord Moreton stripped off his gloves and held his hands out to the warmth. 'It's been the devil of a journey, however. The roads are in a shocking state.'

Despite the reflected glow of the flames, Diane could see that the Captain's face was very pale. His gaze turned once more towards her, then flicked quickly away. 'I assume you found it necessary to—marry her,' he said tightly, 'since you have brought—her—with you.'

'Yes, we were married yesterday. And I regret to say we shall have to go through with the rest of our plan, William.'

'I see. Then your worst suspicions . . . about Diane . . . about her . . . were correct?'

'I'm afraid so. She has admitted the existence of a plot to free Napoleon, although she has been clever enough to confess nothing that the Foreign Secret-

ary hadn't already told me.' There was an infini-
tesimal pause. 'I'm sorry, Will. I know how much
you were hoping that we were all mistaken.'

'It's of no consequence.' The bleakness of the
Captain's expression belied his words. He squared
his shoulders and turned once more to face Diane.
Her heart ached to see the hurt, mingled with
self-contempt, that was reflected in his normally
cheerful features. 'I made a fool of myself, didn't I?
You must have been amused to find your victim
such an easy conquest.'

'No.' Overwhelming fatigue and bitter regret
made it hard to speak clearly, but she forced the
denial out of her aching throat. 'Please, William, I
beg you to believe that deceiving you was never
easy. I hated involving you in Mr Baker's plans.'

'Did you, Diane? But they were not only *Mr
Baker's* plans. They were your plans, too. They
must have been, for you did everything in your
power to make sure they succeeded.' The Captain
drew himself up with youthful dignity. 'You pretended to love me, Diane. You deliberately lied to
me, not just once but over and over again.'

She felt as if every last vestige of colour was
draining from her cheeks. 'It wasn't all a lie,
William, truly it wasn't. I was very . . . I am
very . . . fond of you.'

His smile was cold. 'And I am *fond* of my
favourite spaniel. She is a faithful bitch and
pleasant to have around.' He picked up his great-
coat from the back of a chair and turned to speak to
his brother. 'I believe I am required on board ship.
There is certainly no reason for me to remain here.'

Lord Moreton grasped his brother's arm in an affectionate gesture of reassurance. 'Waste no time in regrets, Will, because there is nothing to regret. You have lost absolutely nothing that was worth keeping.'

'Except my illusions, perhaps.' The Captain fastened the metal frog of his coat collar. 'My Colonel will expect to speak to you later this evening, Edward, when you've had a chance to rest. As you know, the ship sails on the afternoon tide tomorrow. Shall we eat dinner together?'

'Yes, I'll look forward to it.'

The Captain left the room without looking again in Diane's direction. Lord Moreton scarcely waited for the sound of his brother's footsteps to die away before rounding on her, his eyes black with fury.

'I trust you are satisfied with what you have wrought, madam. In addition to all the other sins I can hold against you, you have also managed to break my brother's heart.'

They had been travelling virtually non-stop for nearly thirty hours, and Diane heard Lord Moreton's accusation through a haze of weariness. Her self-control, intolerably strained by the months of deception, finally snapped.

'If the Captain's heart is broken, he inflicted the wound himself,' she said. 'Your brother came to London determined to put his memories of battle behind him. He was more than willing to fall in love with the first presentable female who said a few kind words to him. I happened to be that female, but if it hadn't been me he chose to fall in love with, it could equally easily have been any one of a dozen other young girls making their débuts this year. It is the Captain's pride which is hurt, not his heart.'

'What a very accommodating conscience you have, my lady. The fact of the matter is that you are ill equipped to pass judgment on the state of my brother's emotions. Since it is obvious you yourself are incapable of feeling either pride or love, I don't know how you would expect to recognise such emotions in others.'

Diane felt the unwelcome smart of tears stinging her eyes, and she turned away so that Lord Moreton wouldn't be able to see how his words had wounded her. When she was quite sure that her voice was under control, she spoke quietly. 'I am dizzy with fatigue, my lord, and shall be happy to relieve you of my unwelcome presence, if you will only tell me where I am to sleep.'

'There is a door immediately to your right,' he said. 'I assume the bedroom lies behind it.'

She walked wearily to the door he had indicated and opened it on to the welcome sight of a small bedroom. Lord Moreton's voice halted her on the threshold. 'I shall order food and hot water.'

'Thank you.'

'I shall not see you again tonight, but don't imagine that my absence will give you the opportunity to run away. The bedroom door will be locked, and I shall be sleeping directly outside it.'

She bit her lip, trying to force back a gasp of hysterical laughter. It seemed that these days she always had a retinue of men sleeping in the corridor outside her bedroom. Mr Baker had guarded her

bedroom door in case she ran away from the
Captain. Lord Moreton, presumably, was guarding
her in case she ran to the Captain and pleaded for
his help. Her guardian and her husband had more
in common than they knew: neither of them trusted
her in the slightest.

She heard herself start to laugh. There was a
touch of wildness in the laughter, but she no longer
cared. 'Don't worry, my lord,' she said sarcasti-
cally. 'Your presence won't disturb me in the least.
I am quite accustomed to men lining up outside my
bedchamber while I sleep.'

'I don't doubt it. In this instance, however, you
should remember that there is one very substantial
difference between me and your former suitors. I
have no desire to be admitted.'

Diane slept for thirteen hours, getting up only
when a maidservant pulled back the bed curtains
and shook her awake. A bath had already been
placed in a corner of the bedroom, and another
maid arrived with two copper cans of boiling water
just as Diane reluctantly removed herself from the
cosy comfort of the feather bed. There was no sign
of Lord Moreton, so presumably he had unlocked
her bedroom door before he left.

A delicious breakfast of fresh milk, eggs, ham
and bread was brought up to her, and by the time
she had bathed and sat down at the table in the
private parlour, she felt strong enough to face
whatever Lord Moreton might have in store for
her. She examined the large mounds of food
heaped on the serving tray and smiled with satisfac-

tion. At least Lord Moreton was not planning to starve her into submission.

After breakfast, one of the maids cleared away the remains of the meal, while the other sat down opposite Diane. 'I'm to keep you company,' she said cheerfully, adjusting her plump curves more comfortably to the contours of the armchair. 'His lordship explained to us how you never like to be alone, even for a moment.'

'Did he indeed?' Diane spoke more sharply than she intended, then forced herself to smile at the maid. The servant couldn't be blamed for following Lord Moreton's instructions. 'Well, thank you for staying here with me. Company is always welcome after a long journey.'

When Lord Moreton finally returned to their suite, it was already the middle of the morning. Diane was seated composedly in front of the fire, reading a week-old newspaper. The maid was sewing, humming quietly to herself. His lordship did not seem entirely pleased by the snug domesticity of the scene in front of him. His mouth tightened into a grim line and he dismissed the maid with the briefest of nods.

If he was displeased, he didn't specify the reasons for his displeasure. 'Good morning,' he said to Diane. His gaze flicked over her in a cursory, seemingly uninterested inspection. 'You look— rested,' he said.

'I feel much better, thank you.' With the benefit of a good night's sleep, Diane had decided that determined courtesy, followed by a full revelation of every scrap of information she possessed, was the only way to set about rectifying the hopeless situation she had been plunged into. 'I enjoyed my breakfast,' she added with a shy smile.

Lord Moreton totally ignored the smile. 'Our frigate will sail in two hours. If you are ready, we should go on board.'

'I'm ready any time. I have no luggage.'

'Your belongings have already been stowed on board. They travelled here with my brother's trunks, as was originally arranged.'

She was glad to know that she would not have to journey all the way to St Helena in her wedding dress and, buoyed by the prospect of changing into clean clothes, she walked up the gangplank to the ship with a lighter heart than she would have thought possible a mere twenty-four hours earlier.

They were not greeted by any of the ship's officers, and Lord Moreton led her down only one flight of narrow stairs before turning into a short, panelled corridor. Half-way along the passage, he stopped and inserted a large brass key into the lock of an oaken door.

'This will be your cabin,' he said.

It was a tiny room, but it was attractively fitted with new furniture and shiny brass lamps. The cover on the wide bed was rose brocade and the window curtains over the small porthole were made of the same fabric. 'It's very pleasant,' she said truthfully. 'I expect I shall be quite comfortable here.'

'I'm glad you like it, since you will be spending a great deal of time here.' He didn't attempt to disguise the mockery in his voice. 'You have realised, I am sure, that you will be locked into this cabin for the entire voyage—except for a brief exercise period each day.'

She paled, then turned aside, shrugging off her cloak while she attempted to regain her composure. 'This cabin and I will certainly know each other intimately by the time we reach St Helena,' she said at last. 'How long will the voyage take, my lord?'

'If we are lucky and the winds are kind, we should be there in about eleven weeks.'

'Eleven weeks!' She swallowed hard. 'I hadn't realised the island was so far away.' She took two paces to the porthole and another two paces back towards the door. In those four paces she had covered the entire floor of the cabin. She tried to imagine seventy-seven days and nights locked into this tiny space. She visualised the boat creeping its way across the storm-swept waters of the South Atlantic. The swell of the tide happened to increase at that precise moment, and her imagination took on all too vivid a hue. She clutched her midriff and found herself thinking of the solid ground under the Tower of London with a new-found appreciation of its merits.

'You don't look very happy, my dear. Do you not relish the thought of an ocean voyage? Remember, it is the only one you will ever take, for you will not leave St Helena once you have arrived there.'

She sat down on her bed, sickened as much by the harsh condemnation in his voice as by the increased rocking of the boat.

'My lord, can we not deal together better than

this?' she asked quietly. 'We have to spend many weeks together, perhaps even several months. It will be intolerable if we are constantly at each other's throats. Once I had thought . . . hoped . . . that we might be good friends.'

'In what way do you hope to gain my— friendship, madam?' Lord Moreton's voice was bland, suspiciously bland, if she had only stopped to think about it.

'I want you to trust me,' she said eagerly, reaching her hands out towards him in an unconscious gesture of appeal. 'I want you to believe that I didn't intend to carry through with my guardian's plan to rescue Napoleon. I want you to believe that I will give you all the information I have in order to thwart my guardian's schemes.'

'I am most anxious to trust you,' he said smoothly. 'What *is* your guardian's plan, my dear?'

'I know so little about it,' she admitted. 'But Mr Baker did tell me that an actor, capable of impersonating the Emperor, will shortly be leaving Lisbon, bound for St Helena.'

'A substitution! So that is how they planned to arrange it!' Lord Moreton's breath emerged in a sharp sigh. He looked down at her and, in the dull light of the cabin, she had the impression that his eyes were icily cold.

'That is most useful information, my dear. What reward—other than my friendship—were you hoping to purchase with it?'

She recoiled visibly. 'I don't expect any reward,' she said. 'I told you before that I don't share my guardian's conviction that Napoleon should be freed. The people of Europe, especially the French people, need peace and prosperity, not another twenty years of military glory.'

'And just when did you reach this interesting conclusion, my lady? Not, presumably, when you originally agreed to help Mr Baker with his schemes.'

She pulled distractedly at a loose thread in her wedding gown. 'I gradually changed my mind,' she said, knowing how feeble the explanation sounded even as she offered it. 'At first, I thought too much about honouring my father's dying wishes. Later on, I had more chance to think of the wider consequences of what I was doing.'

'How—sensitive—of you. And are you sure you don't have any other tiny snippets of information you could pass on to me? Remember, there are so many ways in which I could make your captivity on St Helena easier, if you are prepared to work with me.'

'I know nothing more than I have told you, but I believe that, some time during the voyage, I shall receive further instructions. I don't know how the instructions will be passed on to me, but I shall tell you anything I find out, my lord, I promise you.'

She looked up, and this time there was no mistaking the cold condemnation in his gaze. 'That is good news,' he said scathingly. 'Although I would have admired you more, madam, if your loyalty had been a little harder to purchase. It is disconcerting to discover that my brother fell in love with a woman who would sell out the dreams of an entire nation for the sake of a little personal comfort.'

She was infuriated by the angry sarcasm of his words, and her own temper exploded in a white-hot flare of rage. 'From the moment we first met, you have been determined to despise me. Well, my lord, I am tired of your scorn! You twist everything I say; you misinterpret my motives; you condemn my character and my morals! I suggest that you look deep into your own soul and perhaps you will find that you are less perfect than you had imagined. I certainly find you utterly repugnant and I would like you to remove yourself from my cabin immediately!'

He looked at her once more, his own face devoid of all expression. He said absolutely nothing, merely closing his eyes momentarily, as if to shut out a sight he found intolerable, then swung sharply on his heel and left the cabin. She heard the grinding of the key in the lock and the quick firm tread of his footsteps passing along the corridor. Then there was only silence.

CHAPTER
SEVEN

THE SHIP set sail within half an hour of Lord
Moreton's abrupt departure from the cabin.
Neither he nor anyone else returned for several
hours. The dull January light was already beginning
to fade when she finally heard the sound of her door
opening.

A slender, elderly man entered, carrying a tray
of food. He bowed politely before setting the tray
neatly in the centre of the room's only table.

'I am Barclay, my lady, his lordship's valet. His
lordship has instructed me to bring you dinner. I
have done my best to prepare appetising food. I
hope you will find it to your liking, my lady.'

She was so relieved to see another human face
that her smile was radiant. 'Thank you, I'm sure it
will be excellent.'

He inclined his head with great dignity and
turned to leave the cabin. 'Wait!' she called out.
'Barclay, please don't go! Did Lord Moreton say
. . . that is, will Lord Moreton be returning here
this evening?'

'I couldn't say, my lady.'

'I see.' She gestured to a leather trunk stowed in
the only available corner of the cabin. 'Some of my

luggage has already been delivered here, Barclay, but I don't have the keys. Could you open that trunk for me?'

His expression softened slightly. 'I shall ask his lordship, my lady. At the moment, I'm afraid I don't have the keys either.' He bowed once again. 'Please enjoy your dinner, my lady.'

The food was palatable enough and, by the time she had eaten, dusk was already changing to the inky darkness of a winter's night. She waited for the valet to come and collect her tray, but he didn't return, neither did anybody arrive to light the brass lamps. She sat on the bed, her legs curled up under her skirts, and stared out over the foam-flecked blackness of the ocean, feeling her anger change first to fear and then back again into a cold, hard rage. She was tired of being a puppet, she thought, who danced either to the jerks of Mr Baker's commands or to the harsh orders of Lord Moreton. There was no reason for her to submit to the bleakness of the future her guardian and her husband seemed determined to impose upon her. When the ship docked at Lisbon, she would leave and make her escape. Money would present no problem. She had her wedding ring, which it would be a pleasure to sell. She had Napoleon's brooch. She touched her hand to her throat. And she had the delicate pearl and diamond necklace which had once been her mother's. With jewels such as these to sell, she could surely beg and bribe her way across Portugal and into southern France.

The more she considered the practical difficulties of her escape, the firmer her resolution grew. She would not allow herself to be at the mercy of other people any longer. She was only a woman, but she was almost of age and she was determined to take charge of her own life. After twenty years of trying to please other people, it was time to please herself.

She whiled away the dark, lonely hours by planning an idyllic new life in a humble Provençal home. She visualised a white-washed cottage perched on a cliff, caressed by the warm winds of the Mediterranean. Red roses climbed around the door (did roses grow in southern France, she wondered?) and the sun shone permanently on a tranquil, turquoise sea. She would live completely alone, she decided, breeding fat grey goats and woolly brown sheep and refusing to talk to any of the neighbouring gentlemen. At night, she would curl up in a comfortable armchair with a good book. Even a bad book, she thought wryly, would make more entertaining company than most of the people she had met over the past couple of years.

In a brief moment of practicality, hastily dismissed, she did wonder whether she possessed all the skills needed by a successful goat-farmer. She pushed the minor worry aside and turned her mind to happier considerations. Anything, she thought, would be preferable to submitting tamely to Lord Moreton's scornful commands.

She came out of her daydream to realise that, without light or heat, the cabin was rapidly becoming bitterly cold, and she decided to get into bed. It was difficult to undress in the dark, but there was just sufficient moonlight to reveal the shadowy outlines of the furniture. Unless the ship rolled unexpectedly, she was unlikely to bump into anything.

She started to prepare for bed by pulling all the pins out of her hair and placing them neatly on the table next to the dinner tray. She raked her fingers through the loosened strands, but she knew that without a brush and comb she had little hope of taming the wild mass of dark curls.

Without the help of a maid, the removal of her wedding dress presented almost insurmountable problems. It was elaborately styled and fastened down the back with two tiny rows of silken buttons. The buttons completely defied her efforts to undo them. She contemplated simply ripping the dress off, but that would leave her with nothing to wear if Lord Moreton refused to unlock her luggage, so she persevered with the wearisome task. She was panting and flushed with triumph when the dress was finally unfastened and she was able to pull it over her head. The cabin door opened just as she tossed the dress on the foot of the bed. She looked up and recognised the shadowy outline of Lord Moreton.

She snatched her dress off the bed and tried ineffectually to drape it over her bosom, doing her best to look both dignified and in command of the situation. Not surprisingly, since both sleeves were flopping agitatedly beneath her chin, her efforts weren't very successful. 'What are you doing here?' she croaked. She took a firmer hold of the pink silk skirts of her dress and tried again. 'Why have you come back to my cabin at this hour of the night?'

Lord Moreton had brought a tinder-box with him. He busied himself lighting one of the brass lamps. 'I'm tired,' he said softly. 'I am going to bed.'

'Going to bed?' Diane repeated. She blinked, startled by the sudden flare of light from the lamp, and stared stupidly around the cabin. 'Then why are you in here?'

'Because this is where I am going to sleep.'

'You are going to sleep in here?'

'It *is* my cabin.'

'Your cabin?'

He turned and began to take his jacket off. 'I do wish, my dear, that you would refrain from repeating everything I say. It makes for exceptionally tedious conversation.'

She swallowed hard, trying not to see that whiteness of his shirt and the breadth of his shoulders. From the corner of her eye, she saw him reach for his cravat and she spoke hurriedly. 'You cannot sleep in here, my lord. Not possibly. There is only one bed.'

'Fortunately it is quite wide.'

'Quite wide!' She realised she was once again echoing his words, and she spoke quickly before he could make any more cutting remarks. 'However wide the bed may be, my lord, you cannot sleep in it. You must find somewhere else.'

'This frigate, madam, is transporting a regiment of soldiers with a full complement of officers to St Helena. There is no separate cabin available for me. Besides, I prefer to keep a close personal eye upon you.'

He began to unlace the linen fastenings of his shirt, revealing a small section of his chest. Diane stared with hypnotised fascination as she became aware that the faint shadow she could see underneath the white linen was actually hair, growing out of his skin in springy dark curls. Did all men have hair on their chests, she wondered? How very odd it would feel if one ever touched it.

She turned hastily away, pulling the brocade cover from the bed and wrapping it tightly around her shoulders.

'Why do you need to keep an eye on me?' she asked. 'What villainy do you expect me to commit, locked and bolted into a tiny cabin?'

'You exchanged no more than three sentences with my valet, and yet you have already managed to entrance him with your false, beguiling sweetness. If my valet had been given the charge of supervising your captivity, I don't doubt you would by now have been given free run of the ship. It is obviously safer to keep you well away from the ship's officers and crew.'

'You exaggerate my powers of attraction,' she said bitterly. 'Even I cannot seduce a man through an oaken door six inches thick. I think the crew of this ship is quite safe while I am locked away. There is no need for you to add your unwelcome presence.'

He sat down on the room's only chair. 'Perhaps you would help me to remove my boots?' he said, totally ignoring her previous remarks.

She gritted her teeth. 'I will not help you to remove anything. My lord, you have not considered all the . . . the implications of your decision. How can you have our marriage annulled when you have . . . That is to say, when we have slept together?'

Lord Moreton's response was sardonic. 'Your pretence of maidenly confusion lacks conviction, my dear. The mere fact of sleeping in the same room will not prevent me from annulling this marriage. And you flatter yourself if you think you can tempt me to consummate our union. I shall do nothing that threatens my chances of becoming free of you.'

Goaded beyond endurance, Diane whirled round to face him, her eyes flashing fire. 'I am considered one of the most beautiful women in London, my lord. What makes you so sure you are safely immune to my attractions? Only five minutes ago, you suggested that I was capable of tempting any man to indiscretion.'

'You forget, my lady, that I am completely armoured against your charms. I learned early on that your beauty is only skin deep. I require something more than physical attractiveness from my mistresses.'

'I am not your mistress,' she said. 'I am your wife.'

Even in the flickering lamplight, she could see that he turned pale. 'As far as I am concerned, madam, you are a liar and a traitor. Nothing more.'

She was more wounded by his insults than she cared to admit, even to herself, and she reacted unthinkingly. Her hand reached up to lash out at him just as the keel of the boat hit a particularly high wave. She lurched forward, her dress and the brocade cover both slipping off her shoulders as she grasped the edge of the bed in an attempt to steady herself.

A sudden, inexplicable stillness descended on the cabin. She saw Lord Moreton's gaze fix itself on the swift rise and fall of her breasts, and she had the impression that his eyes darkened with some fierce gleam of emotion. Within seconds, the trace of emotion vanished and was replaced by a blaze of white-hot anger.

Diane glanced down in the direction of his gaze and her heart began to beat with real fear. Her brooch, the Napoleonic bee, gleamed in the glow of the lamp, its sting on fire with the striped glow of alternating topaz and diamonds.

Very slowly, Lord Moreton stretched out his hand to remove the brooch, and his fingers brushed against the soft swell of her breast. Neither of them moved, and for several tense seconds his hand lingered on her bare skin. The unfamiliar heat generated by the contact seemed to spread out and envelop Diane's whole body.

She was frightened by the strangeness of the feeling and instinctively she retreated, walking backwards in the direction of the cabin door. She stopped only when her legs were pressed tightly against the wood and she could go no further. In two quick strides, Lord Moreton was in front of her, his arms on either side of her and his palms pressed flat against the door. She couldn't move, or her body would touch his.

With one hand, he reached again for the brooch. The catch was very stiff and it took him some time to unfasten it. The silence in the tiny room was oppressive and Diane felt sure he must be able to hear the unnaturally loud and rapid thumping of her heart. When he finally removed the brooch from the bodice of her chemise, she was shaking from head to toe, even though she wasn't exactly afraid. In fact, she wasn't quite sure what she was feeling.

Lord Moreton looked at her in grim silence, then pressed the tiny diamond at the waist of the bee. The brooch clicked open and the lock of pale brown hair was revealed. He stared at it in silence for several seconds, then his mouth twisted into a bleak smile.

'You promised to tell me everything about your guardian's plans, my lady. I wonder how the significance of this elegant little bauble slipped your mind?'

She felt a wave of hopelessness wash over her. 'What can I say?' she murmured despairingly. 'Will you believe me if I say that in the shock of finding myself married to you, I completely forgot I had been given it?'

'No, my lady. I won't believe such an obvious lie—even though your lips tremble with such a convincing appearance of tragic innocence.'

'Then you must believe what you will, my lord.'

She forced herself to look up and her gaze chanced to meet his. For some inexplicable reason, her eyes filled with tears, and she dashed them

angrily away. When the foolish tears refused to
stop, she turned her head to one side and stared
determinedly away from him, even though she
could still feel the teardrops rolling relentlessly
down her cheeks.

Lord Moreton made a small, harsh exclamation,
quickly cut off, and she heard the brooch click shut
again. Without saying another word, he grabbed
his jacket from the chair and, pushing her to one
side, jerked open the door. It slammed shut behind
him with a force that caused the crockery on her
dinner tray to rattle.

She stood to one side of the door for a very long
time, then walked slowly back to the bed and
crawled under the covers. It was dawn before she
finally fell asleep, and Lord Moreton still hadn't
returned to the cabin.

The ship arrived in Lisbon Harbour a week later.
During that entire time Diane had not seen Lord
Moreton, nor had she been introduced to any of the
ship's officers. Barclay and the Captain were her
only contacts with the outside world.

On the day after the confrontation with Lord
Moreton, Barclay provided her with the keys to her
leather trunks so that she was finally able to change
out of her wedding gown. She folded it thankfully
and stuffed it in the deepest recesses of her locker.
The valet also continued to serve all her meals and
to bring her hot water each morning for bathing.
She was grateful for the calm courtesy with which
he invariably treated her, and actually began to
look forward to hearing the chink of china in the

corridor which heralded his arrival.

Captain Moreton came punctually twice a day in order to take her for a brisk walk around the decks. The winds were high and the salt-laden air bitterly cold, but the sailors she saw during her brief walks seemed to be perfectly cheerful and she concluded that the weather, though rough, was not dangerous.

Her walks with the Captain took place in total silence. The noise of the wind in the sails and rigging effectively precluded rational conversation, but, in any case, the Captain showed not the smallest desire to speak to her—and Diane, burdened with oppressive feelings of guilt, could think of nothing she wanted to say to him. She realised as the week drew to a close that, since her argument with Lord Moreton, she had probably not exchanged more than two dozen sentences with another human being.

Her determination to escape from imprisonment merely increased as the difficulties of her situation became more apparent. It was clear to her that her best—perhaps her only—chance of freedom was likely to arrive when the ship docked in Lisbon. If she could somehow manage to get on shore, she could disappear into the dockside crowds and begin her journey to freedom. Once the ship left Lisbon, it would also be leaving Europe, and escape inevitably would become more complicated.

She was sitting on the bed, her nose pressed to the small porthole in order to watch the activity on the dockside, when Lord Moreton came into the cabin. She scrambled off the bed and faced him with unconscious defiance.

He scrutinised her appearance closely. 'You look—pale,' he said, breaking the long silence.

Her chin inched higher. 'I am a prisoner, my lord. I suppose pallor is inevitable for people who are kept confined against their will.'

His expression hardened. 'Many prisoners would relish the luxuries of your situation. In the circumstances, the terms of your imprisonment cannot be considered harsh.'

'Perhaps not. I dare say the perspective of the gaoler is always different from the perspective of the prisoner.' She turned away. 'Did you come here for some special purpose, my lord? Or did you merely wish to remind me of my great good fortune in being kept so cosily locked away?'

'I came here to say that you are to dine with me tonight. The Marques de Algarve Branca, the most important local landowner, has invited Captain Moreton and his bride to join the ship's captain and some other senior officers for dinner at his house. I shall take the place of my brother as "Captain Moreton", and you are to accompany me.'

'Why?' she asked. 'Why, after seven days of enforced isolation, do you suddenly wish me to take my place among the officers' wives? Why do you want me to accompany you to some Portuguese dignitary's house?'

'Our ship will remain in port for less than forty-eight hours. If Mr Baker and his fellow conspirators want to give you a message before we set sail for Africa, they have only a short time in which to reach you. The invitation from the Marques de

Algarve Branca was the only communication my
brother and his supposed bride received. Therefore, it is logical to conclude that somebody will
attempt to contact you when you are at this
party.'

'I see. What makes you suppose that I won't
betray you as an impostor and claim sanctuary with
the Marques?'

'Only my judgment that you are too wise to make
any such attempt. The ship's officers have all been
alerted to watch you closely, although they haven't
been told precisely why you are to be guarded. The
smallest indication that you plan to betray me,
however, and you will immediately find yourself
surrounded by naval officers, all eager to prove
their mettle.'

'Watching over me will certainly prove a real test
of their bravery. One woman alone, and a dozen
men to guard her.'

'The odds are not in your favour,' he agreed
silkily. 'Just remember them if you should be
tempted to try anything foolish. I'm sure I don't
have to explain how much more unpleasant your
captivity could be if I chose to make it so. Your
exercise periods, for example, could be discon-
tinued. Or the hot water you require for bathing
could be stopped. Or your meals could become—
less bountiful.'

'There is no need to continue with your threats,'
she said bitterly, turning away to stare out of the
tiny window. 'I understand precisely what is required of me. You are setting a trap and I am to be
the bait. If I obey your instructions implicitly, I

shall not be eaten when the trap is sprung. I shall be permitted to return to this ship and remain your prisoner until you need to bait your next trap. You are full of generous impulses, my lord.'

He bowed mockingly, although his eyes seemed to contain a hint of some other emotion. 'I thank you for the compliment, my lady. I believe I have not previously been known for my generosity. Until this evening.' He did not wait for her reply, but turned and went quickly from the cabin.

Diane chose her clothes for the party with a care that surprised her. After a great deal of thought, she selected a cream satin gown, trimmed with a froth of turquoise Brussels lace at the neck and sleeves. The rich lace enhanced the subtle blue sheen of her eyes and the soft colour of the satin flattered the ivory pallor of her complexion. She put on her mother's pearl and diamond necklace and added a pair of drop-pearl earrings, all jewels she had worn for her wedding. Lord Moreton had not delivered her jewel-case to her, so she had no other choice, but she felt confident that these would be sufficient to buy her transportation all across Europe if she needed it.

She had been waiting for almost an hour when Lord Moreton finally returned to the cabin. He was once again dressed in his brother's uniform, and the black silken eye-patch covered his left eye. There was no sign of the real Captain Moreton, who had presumably been banished to his cabin for the duration of the masquerade.

Lord Moreton picked up her velvet evening cape and draped it round her shoulders. He extended his hand and she saw that he held out Napoleon's brooch. 'You may need this to identify yourself to your fellow conspirators,' he said. 'You had best conceal it somewhere about your person.'

'I don't want it.'

'Take it.'

She took it without another word and dropped it indifferently into her reticule. She stared straight ahead of her.

'Are you ready to leave?' Lord Moreton asked quietly.

'Yes. Quite ready.'

They walked in silence up the narrow flight of stairs to the deck. The night air struck chill when they left the enclosed corridors, but in this southern latitude it lacked the bitterness of the London winter winds. The crew scarcely glanced at them as they walked past, well accustomed by now to the sight of 'Mrs Moreton' walking along at the side of the Captain, her husband.

Diane and Lord Moreton descended the gang-plank together, Lord Moreton guiding her steps with false solicitude. She realised during their slow progress to shore how utterly unrealistic her dreams of escape had been. Sailors guarded the gangplank; more sailors patrolled the quayside. Even if—by some miracle—she could have ma-noeuvred her escape from the locked cabin, she could never have left the ship unobserved. She offered a silent prayer of thanks for the Marques de Algarve's dinner invitation. Without it, she would

have had no chance of escape. Because of it, there
was a slim possibility that she might yet find some
opportunity to run away into the welcome blackness of the night.

The Marques had sent carriages to transport
them all to his palace, some miles north-west of the
harbour. They travelled with the Colonel and his
lady, driving through the ornate, mosaic-tiled gate-
way after less than an hour's journey.

It was strange to hear herself introduced to the
Marques and Marquesa de Algarve Branca as 'The
Honourable Mrs William Moreton'. It was even
stranger to find herself treated by Lord Moreton as
a much-loved new bride. His portrayal of devotion
was so convincing that occasionally she needed to
remind herself that the reason he stayed so closely
by her side was not because he loved her madly, but
because he was determined not to let her out of his
sight.

At dinner she was seated next to an elderly
Portuguese nobleman whose command of the
English language was apparently limited to the
phrases 'beautiful lady' and 'wonderful food',
which he used alternately in response to all Diane's
attempts at conversation. The possibility of increasing his powers of response twofold by saying
'wonderful lady' or even 'beautiful food' had
obviously not occurred to him. However, he smiled
with great good humour, and Diane decided that
she had endured many more tiresome dinner companions. Her other partner was an officer of the
Captain's regiment who, despite what Lord Moreton had said earlier about alerting all the officers to

watch over her, did not seem to be paying her any special attention. Having remarked that he was delighted to see she had recovered from her sea-sickness, he returned his attention to the plumply pretty Portuguese girl on his left, who was blushing and giggling as she instructed him in the rudiments of Portuguese grammar.

Finding both her table companions temporarily preoccupied, Diane glanced across the table to the place where her husband was seated. To her sur-prise, she found his gaze fixed upon her, his eyes burning with a seeming mixture of intense longing and blazing passion. For some reason she found it impossible to lower her own gaze, and she felt the heat creep up into her cheeks until she was sure they must be suffused with colour. Yet again she reminded herself that these glimpses of passion in her husband were all false, part of the role he was playing as Captain Moreton. But her body did not seem to respond to the cool, crisp messages sent out by her mind. She trembled with the irresistible urge to reach out across the table and caress the hard line of Lord Moreton's cheek. She could almost feel the tip of her finger brushing across his mouth. She could almost feel his lips descending to capture hers . . . The officer on her left coughed, and she blinked rapidly, tearing herself out of the extra-ordinary daydream. She couldn't imagine what had caused it.

'Excellent dinner, what?' the officer remarked.

'Oh . . . er . . . excellent.' She did her best to pull her scrambled wits into some sort of order. 'The baked codfish was particularly good.'

'Yes, indeed. Not like the food we had when I was here before. That was nearly ten years ago now. Hard to believe it's the same place.'

The conversation continued along its predictable path, with Diane enquiring dutifully about the officer's role in the Peninsular Campaign while her gaze searched the room, trying to decide which of this collection of amiable bores could possibly be her guardian's fellow conspirator. Whoever he was, he had not made even the slightest move to get in touch with her, and she began to feel a tiny relaxation of the tension that had gripped her all evening. Perhaps, after all, nobody was going to tell her anything, and she could make her escape quietly, without feeling obligated to find some way to pass on the information she received. As soon as the ladies withdrew, leaving the men to their brandy, she would search out some unguarded back entrance and run off into the night.

The moment for the ladies to leave the dining salon finally arrived. They rose in a graceful flurry of bright silk and shimmering gauze, following the Marquesa out of the room. Seemingly by chance, Diane found herself walking in step with a middle-aged lady dressed in outmoded grey muslin. She remembered that the lady had been introduced as the Dowager Condesa of somewhere or other, but she had not understood any English, so it had been impossible to converse with her. Not wanting the lack of a common language to present a barrier to friendship, Diane smiled warmly and gestured around the richly-decorated ladies' drawing-room.

'It is lovely here,' she said. 'The silk wall-coverings are very beautiful. *Très belle*.' The Condesa's face remained unsmiling, so Diane tried again. '*Muro bonito*,' she murmured, not quite sure if the words were Portuguese or Spanish—or possibly neither.

The Condesa opened her fan and fluttered it rapidly in front of her mouth. 'Mrs Moreton, you are please to follow me. There is a—friend of mine—who wishes to meet with you.'

'You speak English!' Diane exclaimed.

The Condesa ignored the self-evident truth of this statement and walked rapidly towards the door. 'Please follow me, Mrs Moreton,' she repeated softly.

They soon left the brightly lit main reception rooms behind as the Condesa conducted Diane in silence through a series of increasingly narrow corridors. The walls were stone, damp with the moisture of centuries, and the stone floors were worn to a smoothness that was almost dangerous. The Condesa finally halted outside a small, white-washed wooden door.

'In here, Mrs Moreton, you will meet my friend,' she said.

The Condesa rapped once on the door, then pushed it open. 'You must go in, Mrs Moreton,' she said. 'You are expected.'

Diane walked slowly into the room. She heard the Condesa swing the door shut, locking it behind her, and looked up to see a short, somewhat stout man leaning comfortably against the fireplace.

'Welcome,' he said, in perfect unaccented French. 'I have been looking forward to meeting you, Mrs Moreton.'

CHAPTER
EIGHT

She replied automatically in the same language. 'I would return the compliment, monsieur, except that I have no idea who you are, or why I have been brought here.'

'I am Senhor Carvalho, a good friend of your guardian,' he said. 'Mr Baker asked me to come to meet you when your ship docked in Lisbon.'

'I see. Do you—do you have a message for me, monsieur? I was expecting to hear from my guardian.'

'Perhaps I have a message. We shall see. I wonder if you have anything interesting to show me first, before we discuss these matters further?'

She understood at once that he referred to Napoleon's brooch, but she pretended incomprehension. She needed a few seconds to sort out the confusion of her thoughts.

'I'm sorry, Senhor Carvalho,' she said. 'But I don't understand what you want to see. What could I have that would possibly be of interest to you?'

His glance became impatient. 'I am a collector of antique jewels,' he said finally. 'I was given to understand that you had something particularly fine to show me.'

'Oh! Oh, I see.' She reached into her reticule and produced the bee, unfolding its silken wrapper and clicking open the secret compartment, before holding it out to him on the flat of her palm.

He examined it for a moment in silence. 'It is indeed exquisite,' he said reverently. 'Guard it with your life, Mrs Moreton, for the Emperor will reveal nothing to you if you cannot show him this talisman. Remember, opportunities for private conversation with His Imperial Highness will be few and far between, and we cannot afford to have any opportunities wasted.'

'The brooch will be safe with me, Senhor.'

'Good, good. I am confident it will be.' Senhor Carvalho's manner became briskly business-like. 'I shall be sailing on the brigantine *Colombo*, which leaves here in about ten days. It is an excellent ship, noted for its speed. I don't imagine, however, that it will accomplish the journey as swiftly as your frigate. You will have at least a month, perhaps longer, to familiarise yourself with the island of St Helena before I send word to you of my arrival.'

'How will you send word to me? What shall I have to do?'

'I have been appointed as the new purveyor of provisions for the Emperor's household. As such, it would not be unreasonable for us to communicate over the purchase of some household necessity. On a certain day, it will be arranged for you to have a private audience with the Emperor. During that private audience, the substitution will take place.'

It took a moment of total, blank amazement

before it dawned on Diane that the rather plump, nondescript man standing in front of her was actually supposed to be Napoleon's double. He was the man her guardian planned to substitute for the Emperor! She was so appalled by Senhor Carvalho's obvious inadequacy for the role that, for a split second, she forgot that she didn't want the plan to succeed.

'But Senhor Carvalho, you can't mean that you are to impersonate the Emperor! My guardian claimed that you were an almost perfect double for Napoleon! You scarcely look like him at all!'

There was no mistaking the genuine note of foreboding in her voice, but Senhor Carvalho merely chuckled quietly.

'The Emperor and I are exactly the same height,' he said. 'And our hands and feet match in size. My body measurements duplicate those of the Emperor as they were two months ago, when we received our last despatch from the island. As soon as you arrive on St Helena, you must find out if he has gained or lost weight in the last few weeks, and I will gain or lose the same amount.'

Diane realised that her dismay had been extremely convincing. Senhor Carvalho was smiling at her with almost avuncular condecension, so she continued to look as doubtful as she felt, allowing her brow to crease into little wrinkles of worry.

'It is not only height and weight which make one person look like another,' she murmured. 'There are a hundred other details to take into account.'

'You are quite right, Mrs Moreton. But you shall see that we've thought of everything.' With another little laugh, Senhor Carvalho walked to a corner of the small room. There was a Chinese screen standing there, incongruous among the simple furnishings of the rest of the room.

Senhor Carvalho disappeared behind the screen and, for a few minutes, Diane heard only the sound of his breathing and the soft rustle of fabric. It was probably less than three minutes before he emerged from behind the screen, still smiling slightly.

He had changed his hairstyle and his jacket, and he was also carrying one of Napoleon's famous bicorne hats. He faced Diane, resting one of his hands inside his coat in a gesture made familiar by a dozen etchings and oil-paintings.

She gasped, almost unable to believe the evidence of her own eyes. The superficial changes of jacket and hairstyle already created a startling resemblance between Senhor Carvalho and the Emperor, but somehow the superficial changes amounted to only a small part of the total difference. By the exercise of some near-magical skill, the actor appeared to have rearranged his nondescript features. His eyes seemed larger and more brooding, his lips were clamped in a firm, Imperial line. The hint of sensuality, so much a part of Napoleon's character, was etched into the fullness of his lower lip and the dark gleam of his eyes. The man in front of her, Diane admitted to herself, duplicated every portrait of the Emperor that she had ever seen.

'Now do you see how our substitution will succeed?' Senhor Carvalho asked. 'If you had stopped to think, you would have realised that we couldn't send somebody to the island who already looked like a walking, breathing double of the Emperor.'

'The likeness, Senhor Carvalho, is incredible,' Diane said with unfeigned conviction. She watched as the actor tossed aside the hat and ran his hands through his hair. Before her mesmerised gaze, he returned once more to his previous unremarkable appearance.

A quiet knock at the door was followed by the low sound of the Condesa's voice. 'It is time for you to leave, Mrs Moreton.'

Diane looked towards Senhor Carvalho, who nodded as he gathered up his hat and walked quickly to the Chinese screen. 'Go,' he said. 'I shall be in touch when I arrive on St Helena.'

Diane slipped out of the room, and the Condesa hurried her back along the narrow corridors. 'The gentlemen prepare to rejoin the ladies, Mrs Moreton. We must be quick.'

If she was going to escape from Lord Moreton, Diane thought, now was the only time for her to do it. If she asked for the Condesa's help, she was fairly confident it would be forthcoming. For her own safety, and for the sake of her fellow conspirators, the Condesa would whisk Diane safely away before Lord Moreton even began to suspect what was happening.

But Diane made no plea for help. Unfortunately, having met Senhor Carvalho, she realised that her guardian's plot to free the Emperor had a fair chance of succeeding. Her conscience, a tiresome creature at the best of times, wouldn't permit her to secure her own freedom at the possible cost of thousands of young men's lives.

She shrugged her shoulders in a gesture of resignation. If Lord Moreton insisted on exiling her permanently on St Helena, she supposed she would have to get used to the idea. If Napoleon could reconcile himself to occupying a tiny island instead of ruling an Empire, surely she should find little difficulty in adjusting to the constraints of isolation.

The Condesa indicated the drawing-room, and Diane fixed a bright smile to her lips as she rejoined the chattering group of ladies. She talked and laughed with her hostess and with the officers' wives as if the most troubling thought on her mind was how soon the gentlemen would forsake their brandy and return to the pleasures of feminine company.

The gentlemen arrived only moments after her own return. Captain Fortescue, the naval officer in command of the frigate, reminded his officers that they had been absent from their duties for a long time, and farewells were soon said. Diane thanked the Marques for his hospitality, searching his paunchy features for any hint of complicity in the events which had just transpired within the walls of his palace. There was no hint of such awareness and she marvelled at his powers of dissembling.

The British officers and their wives lined up in the foyer of the Marques's palace and waited for the carriages to arrive. Captain Fortescue and his wife were the first to leave, and Diane found that, somehow, she and Lord Moreton had once again been left to travel alone in the last of the carriages provided by the Marques. She wasn't sure if she was glad or sorry that the need for their masquerade of affection had ended so soon. It was disturbing to think that she enjoyed Lord Moreton's yearning glances and tender caresses, even though she knew they were merely pretence.

The other carriages had passed through the stone pillars that marked the entrance to the palace before Lord Moreton gave the coachman the order to depart. The coach swung into motion and he leaned back, gazing sardonically at Diane. As she had feared, his loving manner disappeared with the slamming of the coach door.

'Well, my lady, I trust you enjoyed your dinner?'

'Yes, thank you, my lord. It was very pleasant.'

Her voice was husky with the weight of unshed tears. Until he spoke, she hadn't realised just how much she had hoped that the emotion he had portrayed during the dinner party was genuine.

There was a little silence, and when he spoke again it seemed as if the words emerged almost against his will. 'You look very—beautiful. Your gown becomes you.'

'Thank you. My dress is new. I haven't worn it before.' Diane pulled her cloak tightly around her as she felt an icy draught of wind blow through a chink in the window-frame. Neither of them was appropriately clad for the chilly night and there were no rugs in the carriage. She stole a glance at Lord Moreton and, deciding that he looked as forthcoming as he ever did, she took her courage into both hands.

'My lord,' she said. 'There is something I have to tell you. Something that happened tonight.'

He was suddenly quite still. 'Yes?'

'I was approached by one of the Marques's guests after the ladies retired to the drawing-room.' She drew in a deep breath, knowing that she was taking the final, irrevocable decision to betray her father's dying wishes. It was several seconds before she spoke, but Lord Moreton said nothing.

'I was taken to meet the man who is to impersonate the Emperor,' she said at last. 'He wanted me to recognise him when we meet on St Helena.'

'If he looks like Napoleon, how could you fail to recognise him?' Lord Moreton's brow creased into a faint frown. 'In fact, why didn't I think of that before? If he looks like Napoleon, we can all recognise him the moment he tries to set foot on shore. I have only to alert the guards.'

'But that is the point, my lord! I don't think you would recognise him. It's the strangest thing. When I first saw this impostor, he looked indistinguishable from a dozen other short men of dark complexion. He then took two or three minutes to change the sweep of his hair and the style of his jacket and—almost before my eyes—it seemed that he was transformed into a living reproduction of the Emperor. Of course, I have never seen Napoleon except in portraits and caricatures, but the resemblance seemed to me to be remarkable.'

'What is the impostor's name, and how is he to get on to St Helena unobserved?'

'His name is Senhor Carvalho and he plans

to travel on a brigantine called the *Colombo*. However, I don't think he will attempt to land unobserved. He has been appointed purveyor of household goods to the Emperor and, as such, has every right to visit the island. Presumably his appointment was approved by the British Government?'

'No doubt.' Lord Moreton asked her several detailed questions, which she answered as accurately and as fully as she could. When she could provide no further information, Lord Moreton looked at her, a curious light in his eyes.

'Why did you tell me so many things I could never have discovered for myself? You must appreciate that I would never have discovered that your guardian's fellow conspirators had made contact with you.'

'That is the whole point, my lord. They are my *guardian's* colleagues, not mine. I have told you several times that I have no wish to see Napoleon set free. He is probably a man of genius, but I don't think this is the right time for his particular talents to be given free rein. The people of France need peace and prosperity. They need harmony with their neighbours, not the empty glory which comes from military conquest. Too many young men have died trying to achieve Napoleon's dreams of a unified Europe. The Emperor came to power because he understood that people cannot live without discipline, and his victories restored dignity and pride to the French people. But he has never understood that national pride cannot fill a hungry stomach or rebuild a devastated village. I want no part in letting such a man loose upon the world once again.'

'You are eloquent, my lady, when you choose to be.' There was a moment's silence before Lord Moreton added, 'It will be invaluable for the British and Portuguese Governments to know that the Marques de Algarve Branca is a Napoleonic supporter. His loyalty to the Portuguese Government had not previously been questioned.'

He had no chance to say anything further. An explosion of sound burst out all around them, shattering the previous quietness of the night, and the carriage lurched so violently that for a moment they were thrown together in a heap on the carriage floor. As Diane lay there, too stunned to move, she heard the shrill screams of terrified horses, followed by the unmistakable sharp crack of repeated pistol-fire.

'What the devil!' Lord Moreton extricated himself swiftly from the huddle on the floor, then helped Diane back to her seat. He was reaching for his ceremonial sword when the carriage doors were pulled open and two masked men burst inside. One of the men clubbed Lord Moreton swiftly over the head. They then seized his arms and dragged him out of the carriage.

Diane had no more than a confused impression of dark, dirty faces and sweating bodies before she, too, was pulled from the carriage and tossed face down on the hard-packed earth by the side of the road. There was no time to break the force of her fall and, for a few moments, the pain of breathing through her bruised lungs was so intense that she could do nothing except lie on the frosty ground, exploring the full extent of her pain.

After a while the agony of drawing breath eased a little, and she began to be aware again of her surroundings. She heard the dull, thudding sounds of fists beating into solid flesh, then the heavy thump of a body landing beside her. She realised that it was Lord Moreton, but she had no way of telling whether he was alive or dead. She could see, however, that his sword had been taken from him.

Painfully she raised her head and inspected the ring of men surrounding her. They all wore masks and were clothed in a tattered array of black garments. Despite her terror, she retained sufficient powers of observation to notice that, beneath the torn clothing, the robbers were all emaciated almost to the point of starvation. Their voices sounded harsh, even menacing, as they conversed in a guttural babble of Portuguese. She felt a moment of blind panic as she considered the full implications of being at the mercy of a group of hostile brigands whom she couldn't understand and who would probably make no effort to understand her.

One of the brigands, who seemed to hold a position of some authority, stepped forward and grabbed Lord Moreton by the hair, propping him into a sitting position against the trunk of a dead olive-tree. Lord Moreton groaned as his head banged against a low branch, and Diane's heart leapt with joy as she became aware that, although he was still only semi-conscious, he was very much alive.

Despite her inability to understand what the robbers were saying, it was evident that the entire band was disconcerted by Lord Moreton's appearance and, from their gestures, Diane concluded that it was the sight of his British military uniform which was causing all the concern. A heated argument soon began among the thieves. One of the men gestured to the Marques's liveried grooms— now lying dead beneath the hooves of the skittery horses—and then back to Lord Moreton's uniform. Diane was quite sure she heard him say the name of the Marques de Algarve Branca. And even without understanding the language, she was sure the name was spoken with loathing.

The brigands' argument, though heated, was brief. At a nod from their leader, most of the men dispersed. One, slightly stouter than the others, walked back towards Lord Moreton and again grabbed him again by the hair. He then beckoned to the robber who still carried the wooden club.

Before she had time to think what she was doing, Diane launched herself protectively in Lord Moreton's direction, throwing herself across his unconscious body as the robber swung his weapon.

'Please don't kill him,' she begged. She knew that none of the brigands could understand what she was saying, nevertheless the helpless words of appeal spilled out.

'There is no reason to kill him, surely you can see that?' As she was speaking, she tore off her pearl and diamond earrings, holding them out towards the silent leader. 'You see, I have jewels. If you will let him go, you may have them, all of them.'

Even as she made the offer, she realised how pathetic it was: the robbers could have all her jewels, whether she offered them or not. They had only to kill her, and then they could strip her body at their leisure. The thought was unpleasantly vivid—she was amazed to discover how little she wanted to die—and she couldn't quite hold back a sob of fear. How could she expect such desperate and hungry men to listen to her, even if they could understand what she was saying? Yet life, even a life of permanent exile, seemed irrationally sweet now that she was in danger of losing it, and, brushing away her tears, she knelt in front of the silent leader.

'Please don't kill my husband,' she whispered. 'We have only been married for such a little while.'

She was disconcerted when she realised precisely what she had said. It was true that she didn't want Lord Moreton to die, but their farcical marriage had nothing to do with that wish. She was merely expressing the common impulses of humanity. The brigands looked at her uneasily, then began to mutter restlessly among themselves, and she glanced up at the brigand leader. He was obviously perturbed by her appeal, even though he had presumably understood none of it. After several tense moments, he barked a curt command to the man holding the club poised over Lord Moreton's head. The robber stopped in his tracks, then allowed his weapon to drop and dangle uncertainly at his side.

The leader pointed towards Diane and gave a couple of crisp orders. She was pulled away from Lord Moreton's inert body and, before she had time even to cry out, he was hit again on the back of his head. She shuddered as she heard the impact of the blow but, when she finally forced herself to look up, she saw that the robber was rubbing his knuckles. She saw that he had used his fist, not his club, so the blow had definitely not been intended to kill.

She was given no time to speculate on the reasons for the comparative mildness of the brigands' behaviour. Two of them lifted her on to a thin brown horse, and one of them sprang up behind her. She gagged as she was assailed by the combined odours of stale sweat, garlic and rough wine. The robber's wiry arms, caked in greasy dirt, reached round her and held her firmly in place as he picked up the reins.

The leader grunted his approval of this arrangement. He freed the carriage horses from their traces and transferred his shabby saddle to one of them. He mounted the prancing animal confidently, and waited while Lord Moreton's limp body was hauled up and draped in front of him. With a flick of the finger, the leader indicated which of the robbers was to have possession of the other horse.

Diane was relieved to see the brigands steal the horses. She doubted if the poor, starving beasts they had previously possessed would have been strong enough to support the burden of Lord Moreton's weight. She was amazed that the wretched creature carrying her and her captor did not stumble. She felt almost as sorry for the underfed animal as she did for herself.

The brigands methodically stripped the grooms of everything they wore, then tossed the naked bodies into the carriage. The leader glanced only once at the pale corpses, then issued a brief, single-word command. The band rode off swiftly into the darkness of the night.

Diane was not blindfolded, but she might as well have been for all she could guess of the route they followed. They turned off the rutted highway and took a path that wound its way through a maze of olive-groves into a sparsely-planted wood. She knew only that the shadowy outline of Lisbon's hills loomed constantly on the horizon and, even when they were deep into the wood, the swell of the hills could occasionally be glimpsed through a clearing in the trees.

The leader called a halt in a deserted clearing. One of the brigands immediately removed his shirt and replaced it with livery stolen from the Marques's dead groom. He tore his discarded shirt into several filthy strips which he braided and used to bind Diane's and Lord Moreton's hands. Both prisoners were hauled off their mounts and led to a rickety shed situated at the edge of the clearing, where their captors dumped them unceremoniously into a pile of straw. From the smell which greeted her as she landed, Diane deduced that they were occupying the previous home of a family of aged goats.

The brigand leader jumped off his horse and walked across the clearing with a definite swagger. He began to talk to Diane, making many gestures towards Lord Moreton's uniform and repeatedly mentioning the word Salamanca. Finally, he turned his shoulders towards her, clutching dramatically at his sleeve, and she saw that beneath years of en-crusted grime his jacket shone with the braided stripes of a sergeant.

'You were a soldier!' she exclaimed, understand-ing at last. 'You fought with the British army at Salamanca?'

'Sergeant. I sergeant. Yessir.' The brigand smiled, displaying a mouthful of black tooth-stumps. He then clutched his heart and panto-mimed a man wounded in battle.

'Are you trying to tell me that you were wounded at the Battle of Salamanca?'

'Sergeant. Yessir. Salamanca. British good. French bad. British soldier save me.'

His command of the English language, however limited, was certainly forceful, but, before Diane could ask him any questions, he launched into another spate of Portuguese. The only phrase Diane understood was the name of the Marques de Algarve Branca, which appeared with monotonous frequency. Seeing her total lack of comprehension, the man swept his arm in a gesture encompassing the entire circle of thieves.

'Soldiers. All soldiers,' he said. 'No food. Marques bad. Marques very bad. No food for old soldiers. No work. No house.' He paused for a moment then added, 'British soldiers not bad. British officers very good.'

Diane offered a silent prayer of thanks to the British army officer who, by saving a Portuguese soldier's life, unwittingly also saved her life and that of Lord Moreton as well. She gave the robber a cautious smile, and he bowed politely before toss-

ing the reins of his horse to an underling and
walking into the goat-shed. With great efficiency,
he proceeded to strip her and Lord Moreton of
every visible item of value except their clothes. The
brigand's sentimental affection for British officers
apparently had its practical limitations.

The brigand made one further concession to
sentimentality. Lifting Diane's hand to remove her
rings, his grimy fingers paused over her wedding
band. With another beaming display of tooth-
stumps, he bowed gallantly and allowed her to
retain it. The flourish of his bow suggested that he
was well aware of his extravagant good nature in
allowing her to retain this cherished possession.

He remounted his horse, dropping the jewels
and coins he had just stolen into his saddle pouch.
'My soldiers go to eat. Very bad hungry. Goodbye.'

'Don't forget to feed the horses,' Diane muttered
as the band fell into straggly order. 'They look as if
they're very bad hungry, too.'

The robbers were just riding out of the clearing
when she finally managed to pull herself to her feet,
no mean achievement with bound hands and a long
gown hampering her movements.

'Wait, Sergeant! Please leave us some water
before you go!' She indicated the lump on the side
of Lord Moreton's head, where a trickle of blood
oozed into a scarlet slash across a darkening black
and purple bruise.

The brigand ignored her, and she pleaded again,
'I beg you, Sergeant. My husband needs water.'

He looked at her in silent contemplation, then
issued a rapid command. Diane was reluctantly

handed a shabby leather container that she judged to be about half-full of liquid.

'Thank you, Sergeant,' she said to the leader. Then she smiled at him and, with little hope of succeeding, indicated her bound hands.

With a grunt, he cut through the strips to release her, and then called quietly to his men. The prospect of unlimited food obviously added a spurt to their movements, for they disappeared quickly into the darkness of the olive-groves and, within less than a minute, the last rustle of the branches had faded into silence.

CHAPTER
NINE

A BRIEF SNIFF of the brackish water was sufficient to
convince Diane that it was undrinkable, but she
poured some of it over Lord Moreton's face, partly
in an effort to revive him and partly in an effort to
remove the dirt and blood from his wound. Even in
the pale moonlight, she could see that the wound
was caked with dirt.

Water alone was not really sufficient to do the
job, and her handkerchief had disappeared, along
with her reticule, into the brigand's saddlebags.
Drips of muddy water trickled off Lord Moreton's
forehead into the folds of his jacket and, with an
impatient exclamation, she pulled up the skirts of
her gown and tore off a strip of her thin muslin
under-petticoat.

She was carefully wiping the congealed blood
away from Lord Moreton's wound when he stirred
restlessly on the pile of straw. With startling
suddenness he opened his eyes.

'Diane,' he said. He reached out wonderingly,
and his hand stroked down the delicate sweep of
her jaw. 'Diane, you're here.'

It was the first time he had ever called her by
name, and her heart gave the strange lurching

movement that she so often experienced in his company. She felt a peculiar, pleasant warmth radiate out from his fingers and flow through her veins.

'Yes, I'm here,' she replied softly. She stretched out her hand, moving it gently over his face, caressing him as he had caressed her. She pushed a lock of thick springy hair away from his wound, and her forefinger traced the line where his hair grew against his cheek.

With an abrupt, almost violent, gesture, he pushed her hand aside and dragged himself to his feet. 'What has happened? Where are we? The men . . .' He pressed his hands to his head, then swung round to face her. 'Who were they? Why have you stayed here with me?'

'I had no choice but to stay,' she said coolly. 'The brigands did not offer to take me to their lair, even if I had wanted to go.'

'The brigands? You did not know our attackers, then?'

She was sickened by the realisation that he still trusted her so little, and she walked to the tumble-down entrance to the shack, looking out into the night so that she wouldn't have to look towards him.

'No,' she said finally, not attempting to defend her answer. 'I didn't know our attackers.'

There was a small, smothered sound from the darkness behind her, and she became aware of Lord Moreton's presence close beside her in the doorway.

'Diane,' he said, his breath feeling warm against

the nape of her neck. 'Will you please untie my hands? Do you think you can manage to do it?'

She turned round to face him as a cloud rolled away from the moon, revealing the stark pallor of his complexion. They walked out of the shack to take advantage of such light as there was, and he leaned against the rickety wall while she struggled with the damp knots of twisted cloth.

It was not easy, and she had plenty of time to tell him what she knew of the brigands as she strove to unfasten the bindings. 'I think they feel particular hostility towards the Marques de Algarve Branca,' she said, as the last knot finally came undone. 'I have the impression that all the soldiers once worked on the Marques's estates, and they resent the fact that he has made no provision for them now that the war is over. They were starving, and simply attacked the first of the Marques's carriages that they felt would be vulnerable. We were a little separated from the other coaches returning to the ship, and so we became victims.'

'Without your intervention, I have no doubt we would have been dead victims,' Lord Moreton said. 'I am—obligated—my lady.'

'A little while ago, you called me *Diane*.'

'I was not in full possession of my wits,' he said curtly. 'I am very thankful, my lady, that you were able to remove your own bindings.'

'No, I could not have managed that, but fortunately the brigand leader cut my bonds just before they rode off.'

'Well, then, we had better start back towards

Lisbon. It is likely to prove a long walk. Do you know in which direction the brigands led us?'

Diane admitted that she had no idea. 'The olive-grove was so bewildering,' she said apologetically. 'One olive-tree looks very much like another to me.'

'Did you not think to look up at the stars?' he asked irritably. 'At least then we might have known the general direction in which we should head. Now we are reduced to stumbling aimlessly through the woods.'

Her eyes flashed turquoise fire. 'I apologise for feeling so happy to be alive that I neglected to insist upon return directions from the brigands. After all, I had merely been thrown from my carriage on to the roadside and held captive by a man who smelled like a warehouse of rancid cheese. True, we had nearly been killed on two separate occasions, but none of that ought to have been a reason for my fluttery feminine weakness to get the better of my common sense. I cannot imagine how I came to be so forgetful.'

'I did not ask for a route-map. I merely suggested that an occasional glance at the sky might have been of help.'

'I'm not a sailor. Even if I had kept my eyes fixed permanently towards heaven, I would not have had the faintest idea where we were going. My education has equipped me to find my way around the *modistes* of London; it has not shown me how to navigate by the stars. Young ladies of fashion are not encouraged to contemplate the wonders of the night sky unless it is depicted on the ceiling of a ballroom. They are certainly not expected to be interested in celestial navigation.'

He turned suddenly and smiled at her, the laughter warming his eyes. 'When you're angry, you talk too much,' he said. 'A most undesirable characteristic in any young lady of fashion.'

The remains of a smile lingered around his mouth, softening the harsh contours of his face. 'But I apologise for being unreasonable.'

His smile sent a shock of pleasure tingling along her veins, and she turned away in an effort to diminish its effects. 'I may talk too much when I'm angry, but you, my lord, are excessively rude even when you're not angry.'

To her surprise, he laughed. He pointed to one of the few stars visible through the covering of cloud, and said, 'This is your first lesson in celestial navigation. That is the North Star. Therefore, if we turn round, we should be going south. And Lisbon is certainly south of us at the moment, so that must be more or less the correct way for us to go.'

'Why must Lisbon be to the south of us?' she asked as they began to step gingerly through the overgrown thickets of trees.

'Because Lisbon is towards the coast,' he said. 'And we have incontrovertibly not travelled inland.'

They did not have to proceed very far with their walk into the woods before they both realised that the task was impossible. The moonlight, frequently obscured by clouds, was feeble even in the clearing. Once they ventured into the woods, all light vanished. Moreover, Diane became aware that her perception of the density of the trees had not been accurate. The brigands knew the overgrown pathways well and had ridden along them confidently, creating a false impression of ease. The bare winter trees had added to the illusion of space but, in fact, the forest was quite dense.

It was Lord Moreton who called a halt. 'We are achieving no useful purpose. Let's go back to the clearing and try to get some rest. At least if we sleep a little tonight, the walk will not seem so wearisome tomorrow.'

Diane was only too willing to agree. In the darkness, she had not been able to avoid the protruding tree-roots and spiky, half-rotten branches. Her satin shoes had been designed for a polished ballroom, not for a rough forest floor, and the soft soles were reduced to little more than shreds of leather tied on to her bruised feet.

They walked back to the clearing, entering the dirty shack reluctantly. The smell of stale goat met them, and Diane looked disconsolately at the heap of damp straw.

In the moonlight, it seemed that Lord Moreton's eyes gleamed with an unexpected hint of tenderness. He removed his thick serge military cloak and spread it over the pile of straw. He bowed to Diane with a mock flourish.

'Your bed awaits you, my lady, and you will be pleased to learn that this establishment prides itself on the softness of its mattresses.'

She smiled, responding to his mood. She poked the collar of his cloak with her toe. 'I trust the pillows have been well aired?'

'Certainly, my lady. We provide only the *best* of service.'

'I can't think how the servants forgot to pack my own pillows. I *never* travel without them.' She sank down on to the improvised bed, her skirts spreading out around her in a billowing pool. She noticed several dozen rents in the stiff silk, and smiled ruefully at Lord Moreton as she picked off the leaves and brittle twigs that were caught in the lace ruffles.

'No pillows, and tattered lace, how shocking! My abigail is falling down on her duties. I think I should hire a new dresser, don't you?'

He drew in a quick breath then turned abruptly away, not attempting to respond to her feeble joke. 'Goodnight, Dia—. . . my lady. I will see you in the morning.'

She was aware of a coldness seeping into her limbs and freezing her heart. 'My lord,' she whispered. 'Please don't go. Don't leave me alone.'

'It will be—better—if I sleep outside.'

She sprang up and clutched his arm before she was aware of what she was doing. 'My lord, it is close to freezing outside, and you have been injured. Your head wound . . .'

Her words died away as she saw how totally he rejected her concern. His gaze remained implacable, his expression so remote that it was impossible to divine his feelings, and she was confused by the strange welter of emotions which suddenly assailed her. It wasn't for his sake, she realised, that she had not wanted to sleep alone.

'Please, my lord, don't leave me by myself,' she murmured. She was suddenly haunted by the memory of a thousand childhood nights when she had huddled in the blackness of her room, while her father entertained a glittering throng of guests in his brilliant, crowded reception rooms. 'It is so dark and cold,' she whispered. 'And . . . and I am frightened when you are not near me.'

For a moment there was absolute silence. Then, with a harsh exclamation quickly cut off, Lord Moreton swung back into the shed.

'Lie down,' he ordered. 'Make yourself comfortable if you can.'

She knelt in the straw, then crawled awkwardly on to his cloak while he watched her with a strange mixture of aloofness and intensity. He waited until she was lying down before lowering himself to the pile of straw. At no point was any part of his body in contact with hers. He did not exactly turn his back on her, but he hunched himself on one side so that Diane could see little more than his shoulder, his ear and the long, muscled length of his thigh.

With extreme hesitation, because something in his behaviour was making her acutely conscious of every action she took, Diane unfastened the ties of her fur-lined cape. The cold seemed to increase by the second and she thought how lucky they were that the brigands hadn't stolen their clothes. The ermine lining of her cloak would have kept the entire band in food for the best part of a month. In the circumstances, the brigand leader had been exceptionally generous.

Keeping her mind on the distant brigands, and thus well away from the extreme closeness of Lord Moreton, she spread out her cloak so that it formed a blanket to cover her. There was a faint rustle from Lord Moreton's side of the straw. She cleared her throat.

'Would you like me to spread my cloak over us both?' she asked his ear, which was the only part of his head visible to her.

'Thank you, but I'm not cold.'

Diane envied him his state of warmth. Her own body felt frozen, at least in those few parts that were not already numb either from exhaustion, pain, or cold. She thought longingly of heated copper warming-pans and thick woollen blankets, and a faint, shivery sigh escaped before she could manage to hold it in.

'What is the matter?'

His voice was brusque to the point of roughness, and she replied quickly. 'It's nothing. Only that I am a little cold.'

He sat up, resting his back against the wall of the hut. He didn't look at Diane when he spoke. 'If you will rest against me, I shall try to keep you warm,' he said. 'Any old soldier will tell you that it's warmer for two people to sleep close together.'

She refrained from pointing out that it was he who had maintained their separate positions, and obediently edged closer to him. Hesitantly, she relaxed her body against his and rested her head against the hard wall of his chest. Even through the thickness of his uniform jacket she could feel the strong beat of his heart. It seemed to her that, for some reason, the beat was rather rapid.

A few minutes passed in uncomfortable silence then, with a small sigh, Lord Moreton put one of his arms around her shoulders. With the other hand he pulled her cloak over them both so that they were tucked into a cocoon of fur-lined warmth.

She wriggled pleasurably as the heat from his body and the heat from her cloak flowed into her from two opposite directions. The icy numbness of her fingers and toes gradually changed into a pleasant, tingling warmth.

'Are you an old soldier?' she asked drowsily. 'I thought you had always been a diplomat.'

'What?' His voice sounded curiously abstracted, in marked contrast to the firm but gentle pressure of his arms around her body.

'You said that old soldiers believe two people can keep warmer if they lie close together,' she explained.

'It is not only old soldiers who have discovered the truth of that claim,' he said. For some reason, his voice sounded very dry. 'Even diplomats have the occasional chance to test the truth of it.'

'Er . . . Have you always been in the diplomatic service?' she asked, conscious of a need to direct their conversation away from Lord Moreton's sleeping habits, although she wasn't sure why.

'Yes, I have always been a diplomat.' After a short pause, he added, 'As a young man, I was sure I would change the face of the world with my brilliant diplomatic negotiations. I imagined myself as the chief architect of a just and enduring peace among the nations of Europe.'

'Most people would say you have fulfilled your dreams,' she said. 'Your reputation in London stands high with everybody, my lord.'

'Does it?' His laughter held more than a trace of self-mockery. 'Now that I am an older man, my dear, I have discovered that diplomacy and justice do not often go together. And rationality certainly has nothing to do with the conduct of any diplomatic negotiation.'

'You are too severe upon yourself,' she said quietly.

'Perhaps.'

She settled herself more comfortably within the protection of his arms. 'Are you going to retire permanently from government service, my lord?'

'I had already retired,' he said. 'I undertook my current mission at the personal request of the Foreign Secretary.'

His current mission. His mission to alert the garrison on St Helena and to leave Diane there in permanent exile. 'I see,' she said. She laughed harshly. 'I had forgotten your current mission, my lord. I had no idea my memory was so bad.'

The warmth drained out of her as she spoke, leaving her limbs chilled and shivery. How could she have forgotten the true state of affairs between herself and Lord Moreton, she wondered? When had reality faded and the wild daydreams taken over? She found that she didn't want to define precisely what form those daydreams had taken, and she stirred restlessly within his arms, uncomfortable with the falseness of the intimacy between them.

His arm clamped her back against his side. 'Don't wriggle. You are letting in a draught.' As though there had been no disruption of their previous conversation, he continued, 'When I return to England, I shall devote all my energies to becoming a better farmer. I have decided that it is more important to increase the yield of my turnip-fields and improve the quality of my wool crop than to worry about the precise boundaries of Saxony, or the taxation system of Moravia. People can eat my turnips and wear my wool. The boundaries of Saxony—wherever we draw them—are simply one more imaginary line for people to fight over.'

Her anger at him drained away. 'You and the other delegates to the Congress offered the Governments of Europe the chance of peace. You cannot blame yourself if some men choose not to take advantage of what you offer them.'

'You are adept at offering reassurance, my lady. And what of your own hopes for the future? I trust they are more exciting than mine.'

She would not tell him that his dreams sounded perfect to her, with their promise of comfortable friendship with village neighbours and close ties to an affectionate family. She thought of the emptiness of her childhood and the long years spent craving for even a casual gesture of affection from her father. She thought of her romantic daydream of finding a man who would offer her all the love and tenderness her father had denied her. She thought of her hope for a family of noisy, laughing, happy children who would never know the torment of a silent house, or the terror of loneliness when the house was crowded with visitors who had no time for a child.

'The French are a practical people,' she said, forcing herself to break the long silence. 'And I am a typical Frenchwoman. I am not much in the habit of dreaming.'

She felt his hand under her chin, tilting it upwards. He looked at her searchingly for a long time, then brushed his thumb gently across her lips.

'Your eyes betray you for the dreamer that you are, my lady. Won't you share any part of those dreams with me?'

Her lips trembled where he had touched them. 'They . . . my dreams are scarce worth discussing. They are very ordinary, my lord.'

'Then share them with me.'

She closed her eyes, yearning to break the barriers imposed by years of indifference from her father. She found that if she kept her eyes shut, it was easier for the words to flow.

'I have lived all my life in the centre of fashionable London,' she said. 'My father felt no urge to possess a country estate, and I have no relatives who live in the country to allow me the chance to visit the English countryside. But I've read so many descriptions of it that sometimes I feel I have experienced the colours and scents of at least a hundred English springs.'

'You have never spent springtime in the country?'

'Until you took me to Plymouth, I had never journeyed more than twenty miles from town.' She smiled faintly. 'Perhaps, however, late January is not the best time to admire the passing scenery.'

'Have you never wanted to visit France?' he asked.

'I don't believe either of my parents was ever reconciled to the loss of their homeland,' she said. 'I was born in England, but of course I have always longed to see the country my parents missed so bitterly. In fact, I have always wanted to travel and see all the other countries of Europe. After the war was over, I tried to persuade my father to travel to the Continent, but he did not wish it. I think he was almost afraid to return to France and find that he no longer recognised the places that were so dear to him.'

'Then Lisbon was your first sight of a foreign city?'

'Yes.' Her smile became a touch rueful. 'I confess that I would have been happy if my first experiences of sight-seeing had been rather more on the dull side.'

'But think of the tales you will be able to tell your grandchildren!'

'If anybody believes them!' She didn't point out how unlikely it was that she would ever have any grandchildren. She preferred, at this moment, not to dwell on the stark reality of a future permanently bounded by the coastline of a small island.

Lord Moreton began to talk quietly about his stay in St Petersburg and, although she was fascinated by his stories, Diane gradually found herself dropping off into sleep. When she woke, it was daylight, and she was alone.

CHAPTER
TEN

SHE RAN to the door, filled with an immense sensation of relief when she saw Lord Moreton crossing the small clearing. She brushed at her unkempt hair and tried unsuccessfully to shake the creases out of her dress, almost grateful that there wasn't a mirror.

'Good morning,' Lord Moreton said as he approached the shed. He was unshaven, but otherwise looked clean and well-groomed. 'How are you feeling?'

'I'm well,' she lied. In truth, every bone and muscle she possessed seemed to be aching.

He walked into the shed, not looking at her closely enough to dispute her statement. 'There's a stream just at the edge of the clearing.' He pointed towards the trees behind the hut. 'The water seems fresh enough to drink.'

'That's good. I'll wash and have a drink before we start our journey back to Lisbon.'

She dipped her arms into the icy spring water up to the elbows, scrubbing off the mud and wisps of straw. She leaned forward to drink and discovered that she had lost all her hairpins, so that her curls fell forward in a tangled mass around her face. She

scraped the curls back into a thick plait and tied it
with a strip of lace torn from her petticoat. She
splashed water over her face until her skin tingled
with freshness, decided there was nothing she could
do about the mud on her dress, and walked back to
the shed.

She found Lord Moreton waiting inside, seated
on the pile of straw. As soon as she entered the hut,
however, he sprang to his feet and held out her
cloak. 'We had better start walking at once,' he
said.

'Yes.' She glanced up at the sun and turned
confidently towards the south-east. 'Is this the correct way?'

He hesitated for a moment. 'It will certainly lead
us back to the harbour. The problem is, we do not
know whether we have been brought north-east or
north-west of Lisbon.'

'I see.' They walked in silence until they entered
the first thicket of trees. 'My lord, do you think the
ship will wait for us? What if she sails with nobody
on board who can identify the impostor when he
arrives in St Helena?'

'We must hope the ship doesn't sail without us.
We had also better walk as fast as we can. Let me go
first, so that I can ease the path for us both. If only
they had left me my sword!'

Passage through the wood was so difficult that
Diane was forced to keep her gaze fixed firmly on
the ground in an effort to avoid the worst of the
hazards waiting to trip her. The remnants of her
shoes disintegrated within the first half-hour of
their march and thereafter most of her attention

was devoted to not thinking about the excruciating pain in her feet every time she stumbled against a tree-root.

So intense was her concentration on her woes that she spared no thought for Lord Moreton's uncharacteristic silence. It wasn't until they suddenly emerged from the wood into the narrow street of a small fishing village that she realised he had not uttered a single word in the five hours they had been walking.

She discovered the explanation for his silence when he stopped at the first of the primitive fishermen's huts and turned reluctantly to face her.

He leaned against the wall of sun-baked mud, sweat beading his forehead. His skin was white, drained of every last vestige of colour, and blood streamed in a scarlet slash from the re-opened wound at the side of his head.

'A tree branch,' he mumbled indistinctly. 'Trying to clear the way and it sprang up and caught me. You go on . . .'

He closed his eyes and slid slowly to the ground. Diane caught him just in time to prevent his head banging on the road. She knelt with his head resting on her lap, wondering how she was to move him. She looked around the deserted street with a hint of desperation in her glance, and then saw that the street was not deserted at all.

Faces of all ages peered from behind the narrow slits that served as windows in the huts. Dark eyes of liquid, mournful brown gazed watchfully and unmovingly at the two of them. After several minutes of silent inspection, a thin, black-clad woman ventured as far as the door of her hut.

Diane did her best to look harmless and respectable, which she knew was somewhat difficult since she was clothed in a satin gown liberally scattered with twigs and spiders.

'My husband has had an accident,' she said, aware that the villagers wouldn't understand her, but unable to think of any other way to break the suspicion-laden silence. 'Can you help us, please?'

The woman who had been brave enough to peep out immediately disappeared back into the darkness of her hut and the rickety wooden door was slammed shut. As if obeying some hidden signal, all the other eyes simultaneously disappeared from the window slits.

It was only a few seconds, however, before the peering faces reappeared. Two or three women walked as far as their doors and, when nothing untoward happened, ventured out into the street. Soon a whole cluster of women and children were gathered around Diane and the still unconscious Lord Moreton.

Diane gave the assembled women her best effort at a placatory smile. The villagers merely stared at her with increased suspicion, making no move to help her or Lord Moreton. 'My husband has been set upon by thieves,' she said, pointing to his wound. 'We need to eat and rest before we proceed to Lisbon. Can you help us, please?'

If the villagers had been quiet before, her words for some reason inspired them to a positive cacophony of eager voices. She could not understand a single word, and eventually the noise died away and the two groups were left staring at each other in renewed, incomprehending silence. Lord Moreton chose this moment to regain consciousness. He gave a hollow moan, stirred, and looked up to find Diane and twenty-odd villagers all staring at him expectantly.

He rubbed his hand across his eyes. 'Am I supposed to know what to do next?' he murmured to Diane.

'Unless you speak Portuguese,' she said dryly, 'I think one of us is going to have to start playing charades.'

'God forbid!' Lord Moreton dragged himself to his feet. He was still pale, and he swayed ominously when he moved away from the support of the wall, but he did manage to remain upright. Only Diane, looking anxiously at the greyness of his complexion, was aware of how much effort it cost him.

'Er—English . . . *Ingles*,' he said to the villagers. '*Navio* . . . er . . . *nosso navio a Lisboa*.'

'Oh, well done!' Diane exclaimed. 'I had no idea you could speak Portuguese!'

'I can't.' His mouth twisted wryly. 'I'm afraid you have just heard the ultimate limits of my command of the language.'

Unfortunately the villagers did not seem to be as impressed as Diane was with Lord Moreton's valiant effort to communicate. They shuffled their feet and continued to look bewildered but, after many repetitions of the words *Lisboa* and *navio*, one woman pointed hesitantly towards the southeast, adding a few phrases of explanation as she pointed. Lord Moreton looked grim as he listened, and even grimmer as he translated the village woman's words for Diane.

'I think she says Lisbon is very far away from here. She can't give an accurate estimate of the distance but, if I've understood her correctly, she says it's almost a day's walk.'

'But how could we have travelled so far?'

'The Marques's palace is about twelve miles north-west of Lisbon—remember it took us well over an hour to reach it. The brigands, I think, must have carried us another few miles west and we compounded the error by travelling west as well as south when we crossed through the woods. I estimate that we are more than ten miles from Lisbon harbour, even though we have reached the coast.'

'Ten miles!' Diane contemplated walking another ten miles in her bare feet, and felt her heart plummet straight to the ground. She leaned tiredly against the wall of the cottage. 'Could we eat first, do you think?'

He smiled, his dark eyes unexpectedly tender. 'I'm sure we could, at least if the villagers have any food.'

He turned to speak to the village women. There was considerable conversation, accompanied by much gesturing and waving of hands, before Lord Moreton finally turned back to her.

'I'm afraid they want your wedding ring before they will take us into one of their cottages,' he said. 'I have offered them my cloak, but they aren't interested.'

'Of course they can have my ring.' She removed

it quickly, surprised by the sharp pang of regret she felt when one of the fisherwomen snatched it greedily. The woman tested it against her broken teeth, before grunting in apparent satisfaction and tucking it into the folds of her rusty black skirt.

'Anna Maria,' she said, pointing to herself as soon as the ring was safely away. She seemed to have no interest in learning their names. She swung on her heel and with quick, flapping gestures indicated that they should follow her down the narrow street.

The business of the afternoon had apparently been concluded to the satisfaction of the villagers. The women and children didn't follow the visitors, but retired to their huts, and the street was soon deserted.

Diane was agreeably surprised when Anna Maria halted at the cleanest and most prosperous-looking of all the cottages in the village. She beckoned them inside, then conducted them on a tour of her home, proudly displaying the fact that the cottage boasted three separate rooms: a stable for the animals, and a bedroom, as well as the kitchen.

There was no need to understand Portuguese in order to know that the bedroom was Anna Maria's pride and joy. A large straw pallet, covered with knitted blankets, was raised on a solid wooden bed-frame, and the floor itself was tiled with some sort of red flagstone, unlike the kitchen floor which was made of compressed earth. Anna Maria's chest swelled visibly as she displayed the colourful blankets. She was obviously inordinately proud of the

fact that she and her husband possessed furniture
and linen, as well as the luxury of a mud-and-stone
wall between the kitchen and the bedroom. She
gave a final fond smile as she patted the mattress,
inviting Diane and Lord Moreton to sit down.
Diane sat, doing her best to look suitably impressed, although the smell of goat and donkey
wafting in from the stable detracted somewhat
from the pleasure of resting her feet.

Lord Moreton looked at her with undisguised
amusement. 'Don't wrinkle your nose,' he said. 'It
was aristocratic sniffs like that which cost your
ancestors their heads. I don't want to offend our
hostess before we eat dinner.'

'Do you . . . do you think we shall have to eat one
of the goats?'

'I'm sure they're much too valuable to kill for our
supper, and I saw no goat-meat hanging in the
kitchen as we passed through. Don't worry about
it.'

To Diane's relief, Lord Moreton proved correct.
Anna Maria's husband, Paulo, returned from his
day's fishing in time to toss a large codfish into the
simmering pot of vegetable stew. It bubbled among
the peppers and black olives, covering the odour
of animals with the enticing smell of hot, spicy
food. Diane's stomach began to rumble in happy
anticipation.

The kitchen table was generously sized, and had
roughly-carved benches on either side of it. Anna
Maria and Paulo sat on one bench together with
Diane and Lord Moreton. Six smiling children, the
eldest no more than ten, the youngest barely able to

walk, seated themselves along the other. The children's clothes were filthy and their hair matted with grease, but Diane saw that Anna Maria made them all wash their hands and faces before they sat down. They all looked a great deal more cheerful than she had ever felt as a child.

Anna Maria set the tureen of stew in the centre of the table and Paulo opened the top half of the door between the kitchen and the stable. The donkey, obviously familiar with the family routine, immediately stuck his head through the opening. Despite his best efforts, however, his muzzle didn't quite reach the table and he watched the progress of the meal with a melancholy, but avid, interest.

His interest was not in vain. When all the bowls had been filled, he was awarded the head of the codfish. He ate it quickly, with every appearance of total enjoyment, then spent the remainder of the meal rubbing his nose contemplatively against the wooden door-frame. While they ate, the children often leaned back and gave him an absent-minded but affectionate scratch. In return, the donkey nuzzled their necks and occasionally blew gently in their ears.

Despite the pungent odours of the stable, Diane thought that the fish stew, washed down by a coarse red wine, was the most delicious food she had ever eaten. She only wished there had been some bread available so that she could mop up more of the sauce. As for the company, she decided, it was a great deal more congenial than that found at most London dinner parties.

The sun was beginning to set before the meal was

over. Now that her stomach had stopped growling, Diane was able to take a fresh interest in her surroundings and, glancing at Lord Moreton, she saw that he looked far from happy.

'Didn't you enjoy the stew?' she asked.

'Yes, but I'm worried about our journey to Lisbon. Twenty miles is a long way to walk, and it's getting dark.'

'Perhaps they would sell us the donkey in exchange for my cloak. It's lined with ermine and must be worth many times the value of the donkey.'

'To us, perhaps, but not necessarily to them. However, there is no harm in trying; they might be willing to make the exchange.'

He began to talk with Paulo and Anna Maria. Diane leaned back against the kitchen wall, allowing the meaningless words to ebb and flow around her in gentle waves. She closed her eyes, feeling the blissful languor of repletion steal up and overtake her. She took another sip of the red wine, and wished that she and Lord Moreton did not have to set out for Lisbon. The problems of reaching their ship and keeping Napoleon safely imprisoned on St Helena seemed remote and unimportant.

A rising spiral of voices alerted her to the fact that Lord Moreton's discussions were not going smoothly. Reluctantly, she opened her eyes.

'Won't they sell us the donkey?' she asked.

'Yes, although they're not happy about it. The real problem, as far as I can gather, is that there is no marked road between here and Lisbon. Somebody will have to guide us from here to the city, and nobody is willing to leave the village after dark.'

'*Gatunos! Ladrãos!*' Anna Maria nodded her head vigorously.

'She claims there are thieves,' Lord Moreton translated curtly.

'*Ladrãos violentos!*' interjected Paulo.

'Well, we have proof positive that they are both right,' Diane said wryly. 'The thieves were certainly violent. What must we do, my lord, if they won't guide us back to the city?'

He paused for a moment before replying. 'Anna Maria wishes us to spend the night here,' he said finally. 'I believe her husband is willing to act as our guide if we wait until dawn before leaving the village.'

'But our ship sails on the dawn tide,' she said. 'We have to be in Lisbon before then!'

'If we are attacked and killed, there will be nobody to pass on the information. If we wait until tomorrow morning, we should arrive safely in Lisbon by nightfall. I can hire a boat to catch up with the frigate.'

'You have no money.'

'I shall simply approach the British ambassador. There will be no difficulty in acquiring funds once we are in Lisbon.'

Diane yawned. 'I'm delighted to hear we are staying,' she said. 'What do you think we would have to offer Anna Maria for the loan of her bed? We are getting short of items to sell, and I had no idea a straw pallet could look so appealing.'

'She has already offered us the use of her bed,' he said brusquely. 'Your wedding ring apparently bought us that privilege.'

'That is excellent news.' Diane yawned again. 'I'm so sleepy,' she added. 'Can we go to bed right away?'

There was a tiny pause. 'You go ahead,' he said finally. 'I am not tired at the moment.'

Diane yawned. 'You must have the consitution of a gladiator, my lord!'

He laughed, but his laughter sounded grim. 'Something like that, I suppose.' He got up from the table, pushing back the bench with a quick, jerky movement. 'I will see if our hostess can be persuaded to provide you with some hot water. I'm sure you'd like to wash.'

'It would be wonderful,' she agreed.

Lord Moreton began the lengthy task of miming the need for hot water, and Diane made her way to the somewhat chilly tranquillity of the bedroom. All six children followed her out of the kitchen, seating themselves on the red-tiled floor and watching with solemn interest as she removed her shoes and stretched out on the straw mattress. As soon as she was settled, the youngest child clambered up on the bed, smiling sleepily as he curled into a tight ball on her lap. He stuck his thumb into his mouth, sucked noisily for a couple of minutes, and soon fell asleep. The other children, emboldened by Diane's willing acceptance of the baby, walked over to the bed and gingerly stroked the satin skirts of her dress. The eldest girl, her dark eyes glowing with pleasure, ruffled the soft falls of turquoise lace, smiling as the filmy material rippled through her fingers.

Anna Maria arrived only minutes later with the

promised bucket of water and, clucking sharply at her children, thrust the sleeping baby into the eldest child's arms. Her offspring did not seem noticeably chastened by her sharp words and clattered out of the bedroom, casting cheerful smiles towards Diane as they went. Despite her fatigue, she was sorry to see them leave. The baby had been especially appealing, she thought. He had felt so warm and soft against her body, so pleasantly heavy as he nestled trustingly in the crook of her arm.

Anna Maria set the wooden bucket down on the floor and rummaged around in the small painted chest, which was the only other piece of furniture in the room apart from the bed. She eventually extracted a threadbare cotton towel and a piece of pumice-stone, putting them on the bed and indicating with a smile that she was ready to help Diane out of her gown.

Until that moment Diane had not given much thought to the fact that she and Lord Moreton would be sharing a bedroom. Excessive modesty would, in any case, have seemed out of place since she and Lord Moreton had spent the previous night curled up under her cloak in an abandoned goatshed. Indeed, her only conscious thought about Anna Maria's bedroom had been that it provided a marked improvement in the standard of their sleeping accommodation. Now, however, she suddenly visualised herself in the candle-lit bedroom, lying next to Lord Moreton, clad only in her muslin chemise. She thought about his hand touching her naked shoulders. She thought about his arm brushing against her breasts, and a flush of burning heat swept over her body, warming her from scalp to toes. As soon as she realised precisely what she was imagining, she jumped off the bed and walked swiftly towards the bucket of hot water.

'There is no need to take off my dress, thank you,' she said to Anna Maria, wondering how on earth she could explain—in mime—her desire to wash and sleep without removing her clothes. She made a vigorous attempt to convey her meaning, but gave up in view of Anna's blank incomprehension.

'I intend to sleep in my clothes,' she said with all the firmness she could muster. 'It's better that way. More comfortable. Yes, that's it. It's warmer, you know.' She smiled—she hoped convincingly—and clutched her arms around the embroidered waistband of her gown.

Anna Maria naturally paid not the slightest attention to these remarks. Moreover, she clearly saw no reason to waste her time in a pointless struggle to understand why the English lady kept clutching her midriff. As soon as she was sure that Diane had stopped speaking, she gave her guest another beaming smile and proceeded exactly as though nothing had been said, and exactly as though Diane were not frantically flapping her arms in a hopeless attempt at communication. She calmly unfastened the row of cream silk buttons at the back of the gown and, with sublime indifference to Diane's continued mumbles of protest, then eased the dress off and pointed commandingly to

the bucket of tepid water. Meekly, Diane knelt and
began to scrub herself clean.

As she rubbed the scratchy pumice-stone over
her arms, Diane reflected wryly that, even if she
had spoken fluent Portuguese, it would have been
difficult to explain to a down-to-earth peasant
woman why she wanted to go to bed clad in an
embroidered gown. Satin stiffened with six rows of
whalebone and liberally daubed with mud hardly
made the most comfortable of night attire.

Anna Maria watched as she finished drying herself on the cotton towel, and then, with a triumphant flourish, produced a tortoiseshell comb
from her apron pocket. With the firmness of a
woman accustomed to dealing with six active children, she pushed Diane into a sitting position on
the end of the bed and swiftly unplaited the thick
braid of her guest's hair. She crooned admiringly as
the lush curls were released from confinement, and
hummed to herself as she began upon the time-
consuming task of unsnarling two-days'-worth of
tangles.

The job was only half done when they both
became aware of Lord Moreton's silent presence in
the bedroom doorway. Diane looked up and, meeting the compelling intensity of his gaze, found
herself unable to look away.

He, like her, must have been provided with a
bucket of water, for there was no longer even the
slightest trace of dust remaining on his face or
around his wound. He had removed his uniform
jacket, presumably in order to wash, and he now
carried it slung carelessly over his shoulder. His

cravat dangled untied against the once-white folds of his shirt-front. He had been unable to shave, for the stubble of his beard gleamed darkly against his newly-washed skin. Diane found herself wondering what it would be like to feel that rough stubble moving beneath her fingertips . . . against her cheek . . . against her mouth.

She was horrified by the extraordinary direction her thoughts kept taking and she tried to look away, but a sudden flare of emotion in Lord Moreton's eyes held her hypnotised. Her stomach muscles clenched in a strange nervous excitement, and the sensation, instead of being disagreeable, was curiously pleasant. She felt sure that her cheeks were aflame with colour although, when she instinctively crossed her arms over her breasts, her fingers seemed icy cold against the heat of her skin.

She realised that Anna Maria had stopped combing her hair and was holding out the comb to Lord Moreton, babbling a stream of Portuguese as she did so. He advanced slowly into the bedroom, accepting the comb as he paused in front of Diane. She clenched her hands in her lap and stared fixedly at her knuckles. Whereas a few seconds before she had been unable to tear her gaze away from him, now she found it impossible to meet his eyes.

At the edge of her vision she was aware of Anna Maria scuttling from the room, taking the wooden bucket with her. Dimly she registered that the woman had paused in the doorway to say goodnight, and she forced herself to look up and wish her a safe night's rest. Anna Maria responded with a black-toothed grin and a respectful bob, closing the door behind her without releasing her hold on the bucket.

There was a lengthy moment of silence, and then Lord Moreton cleared his throat. 'Paulo and the children wanted to roll out their pallets and get to bed. I could not stay in the kitchen any longer.'

Diane returned to the obsessive inspection of her knuckle-bones. 'I quite understand,' she said. She searched desperately for something else to say, but her mind remained an unco-operative blank.

Once again it was Lord Moreton who broke the uncomfortable silence. 'Would you like me to finish combing your hair? I see that Anna Maria has not quite completed the task.'

'That would be very good of you.'

'Not at all.'

Lord Moreton made a few swift passes of the comb through the front of her hair, then cleared his throat again. 'I believe I shall have to sit on the bed in order to reach the back of your hair. That is where most of the tangles remain.'

Diane looked studiously at the mud-filled cracks in the stone wall. It was as good a way as any of avoiding looking at him. 'Then by all means sit on the bed, my lord. Or I could stand up.'

'There is no need for that,' he said somewhat brusquely. He sat beside her and she bent her head, glad that the heavy sweep of her hair hid the scarlet glow of heat burning in her face. She had never been responsible for taking care of her own hair; one of the maids had brushed it twice a day ever since she could remember. But their ministrations had never caused a tight steel band to coil itself around her rib-cage, making it difficult to breathe. Their actions had never made her tremble inside, or made her hands icy cold even while the surface of her skin seemed to burn with fever.

Lord Moreton lifted up the weight of her hair and ran the comb through the tangle of dark curls that rested against her shoulders. His breath was warm against the bare nape of her neck, and her own breathing came to a precipitous halt as his fingers twisted softly in the thickness of her hair.

With a great effort of will, she shook off the strange languor that afflicted her. It was ridiculous that the simple act of brushing her hair should leave her feeling so disoriented. 'I think my hair is free of tangles now, my lord,' she said breathlessly.

'No. There is one section I have not yet combed.' His voice was curiously thick, and for a moment the comb scraped clumsily against her shoulders.

'I'm sorry,' he said curtly.

'It's quite all right, my lord. You didn't hurt me.'

'Did I not?'

This time there was no mistaking the strange inflexion of his voice, but he resumed his careful combing of her hair, and the debilitating weakness overcame her again, precluding the possibility of rational thought. It seemed to her that there were no sensations left in the world except the featherlight touch of his hands against her skin and the warm whisper of his breath caressing her shoulders.

The movement of the comb through her hair finally stopped and a great silence filled the space between them, growing and thickening until the air vibrated with a tension that she could almost touch.

'Diane . . .' She hardly heard the murmured sound of her name as she felt the slow, deliberate caress of his hands over the slope of her shoulders and then—unbelievably—the pressure of his fingers as they curved round the aching fullness of her breasts, gently pulling her into his arms.

A lightning flash of sensation ripped through her entire body, radiating from the place where his hands cupped her breasts. The sensation was so sharp, so acute, that she felt it almost as pain, and she sprang off the bed, terrified by the unfamiliar power of her own feelings.

'Th-thank you for combing my hair,' she stuttered. 'It is completely free of tangles now. It is enough, my lord.'

'No,' he said harshly, and even in her over-wrought state she could hear that his voice was flat with the effort of control. 'No, Diane, it is not enough. It is nowhere near enough for me.'

In two strides he had crossed the tiny room, taking her back into his arms as he urged her to turn around and look at him. 'I want to make love to you, Diane. I have been in torment ever since I first met you. Oh God, I feel as if am being torn apart with the need to hold you in my arms!'

She did not dare to look at him, so she once again stared blindly at the wall. She knew that, for the sake of her sanity, she had to refuse him. And she also knew that if she once looked at him, her power to refuse him anything would be lost.

'My lord, we cannot make love . . . We must not . . . It is not right . . .'

'We are husband and wife,' he said softly. 'How can it not be right?'

'But our marriage is not real, my lord!'

'Tonight we shall make it real. Let me love you, Diane. Let me show you how it can be for a man and a woman when they make love.' With one finger he traced the quivering outline of her mouth and then, while her lips still tingled from the touch, he bent his head and kissed her.

She had never known, never even imagined, that the mere touch of a man's lips to her mouth could have such an effect upon every part of her body. She felt as if her limbs were dissolving until there was nothing left of her except a fierce ache of longing and the feverish union of her lips with his. She reached up her arms, winding her hands in the springiness of his hair as she had so often longed to do, and she felt his body shudder convulsively against hers. His hands tightened against her back, his mouth moved urgently over hers and suddenly, shockingly, she felt the hard thrust of his tongue against her lips.

She immediately pulled away, frightened both by the erratic thudding of her heart and by her sudden inexplicable urge to open her mouth and accept the thrust of his tongue against her own. She felt confused, almost disembodied, and yet at the same time startlingly aware of every inch of her skin. And every inch of it seemed to be crying out for contact with Lord Moreton.

Once again, the silence between them stretched out interminably. It was shattered by the sudden echoing trumpet of Paulo's snores, and Diane gave a tiny gasp of laughter that teetered perilously close to a sob. Lord Moreton's eyes darkened with wry, momentary amusement, then he framed her face in his hands and looked at her searchingly. He brushed a kiss of butterfly lightness across her mouth.

'There is nothing to fear, Diane,' he said. 'We have all night ahead of us and I swear that we shall do nothing that you do not want.'

'My lord . . .'

'My name is Edward,' he said huskily. 'Let me hear you say my name.'

She looked up at him and the tenderness she saw in his face caused her fear to vanish as if it had never been. 'Edward,' she whispered. 'Will you please kiss me again?'

He drew in a quick, unsteady breath, then swept her into his arms and carried her over to the bed. He cradled her against his heart as he covered her with the thin knitted blanket, and she could feel the shudder of his body against her side.

'Why are you trembling?' she asked. 'Are you cold?'

He laughed softly. 'On the contrary,' he said. 'I believe I am burning up. I am on fire, Diane, and only you can extinguish the blaze.'

Even in the flickering light of the single tallow candle she could see that all trace of tenderness had already vanished from his eyes. His gaze now reflected the same feverish glitter she felt within herself, and his cheeks were stained with a hectic flush of desire. She realised that he held himself under the most rigid control, and she was suddenly seized by the longing to know what he would be like when that iron self-control finally snapped.

She supposed that Paulo was still snoring and that the animals still snickered in their stable, but she was deaf to the outside world. She could hear only the sound of Lord Moreton's rapid breathing and the thudding pound of her heart.

She held out her arms, welcoming him into her embrace, and he gave a low groan as his lips covered hers in a passionate, seeking kiss.

His hands stroked away her clothes and turned her body to flame until, at last, the world faded away into a dream of dark fire and there was nothing left but the feel of his hard body coiled tight against hers, and the blissful, mindless ecstasy of his possession.

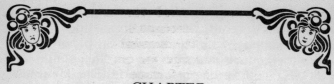

CHAPTER
ELEVEN

IT WAS Paulo who woke them shortly before dawn
the next morning, summoning Lord Moreton into
the kitchen to wash and dress while Anna Maria
came into the bedroom to help Diane braid her hair
and do up the buttons on her gown. They all met in
the crowded kitchen, where they drank a cup of
warm goat's milk and bade goodbye to the sleepy-
eyed children.

Diane, noticing the yearning gaze of the eldest
daughter, tore off long strips of the turquoise lace
edging her gown and gave it to the child, exchang-
ing a rueful smile with Lord Moreton when the
tattered lace was accepted in a stunned and
gratified silence.

The younger children began to cry when they
realised that their donkey was about to be taken
away from them, but Lord Moreton quietened
their tears by explaining, in halting Portuguese,
that the animal would be returning the next day
with their father. The cherubic, milk-smeared faces
were immediately full of smiles, and the donkey
was smothered in sticky farewell kisses.

Anna Maria was almost as full of smiles as her
children when they said their final goodbyes. 'And

so she should be,' Lord Moreton muttered to Diane. 'She obviously missed her calling. Anybody who can negotiate the acquisition of an ermine-lined cloak in exchange for one day's hire of a donkey could make a fortune in a major trading city.'

'But in fact we probably need the donkey more than she needs the ermine,' Diane pointed out. 'Besides, it doesn't matter. It is not all that cold.'

'You were never a very good liar,' he said softly as he lifted her up on to the donkey. 'It is not very convincing if your teeth chatter when you claim to be warm. Here, take my cloak.'

'But my lord . . .'

'Last night you called me Edward,' he said, as he fastened the cape securely beneath her chin. 'And I have found that I like the sound of my name on your lips. Do you know that you have just the tiniest, lingering trace of a French accent?'

'I have never been told that before.'

'Ah, but nobody else has had the opportunity to hear your say *Edward* in precisely the urgent, longing way that I have heard you say it.'

She blushed furiously, but there was no chance to say anything more, for at that point Paulo finished his lengthy instructions to his children and gave the donkey a hearty slap on its rear. It snickered once in protest, and then set off in a steady, albeit somewhat reluctant, walk. Paulo and Lord Moreton walked briskly alongside the animal.

Once they had left the village, the hard-packed dirt road soon degenerated into a winding track.

Within a mile, it became increasingly narrow and hard to walk along. Diane realised that the villagers had not exaggerated when they claimed it would be impossible to follow the track at night. They were also correct in claiming that it would be impossible to find the trail for Lisbon without a guide, for the main route was criss-crossed with wandering side-tracks, and at the points of intersection there rarely seemed any way to decide which path was the main one.

To compound the miseries of their journey, the wind brought with it gusts of intermittent rain that turned stretches of the dirt road into muddy quag-mires and soaked their clothes until they became sodden masses of half-frozen fabric.

Diane glanced frequently at Lord Moreton, wor-ried equally by the grimness and by the pallor of his expression. She hoped—how desperately she hoped—that the grim set of his features was caused by concentration on the task of reaching Lisbon, and not by regret for what had occurred between them the previous night.

Ever since she first met him, she had fought against acknowledging that she was falling in love. But now, having spent the night in his arms, there was no longer any hope of disguising the truth from herself. She loved him, hopelessly and irrevocably. The rational part of her brain tried to point out that her love alone could not turn her marriage with Lord Moreton into a true union. But try as she might to temper her fantasies with caution, her heart would not co-operate with her head. As the donkey slowly jogged out the miles, her imagination soared above the miseries of the chilly road to take comfort in a glorious daydream.

In this wonderful dream, when they arrived back at the ship, Lord Moreton ignored the frantic questions of the waiting officers and crew. He hurried to their cabin where he swept her into his arms and declared that he loved her. He kissed her passionately, his body hard and demanding against hers. Then he ripped off her clothes . . . The next entrancing stage of her fantasy kept Diane warm and glowing for several freezing miles of their journey.

Unfortunately, try as she might to prevent it, the coldness of reality eventually intruded on the rosy edges of her dream. Even if he loved her, Diane thought, what could their future hold? How could they remain together? Lord Moreton was a nobleman with obligations and responsibilities he could never escape. Her future lay on a barren, hot island in the South Atlantic. His future lay in England, in the lush green tranquillity of the countryside. If anything could be certain in life, it was that he did not need a suspected traitor as his bride.

A touch of bitterness tinged her smile as she realised the monumental foolishness of her dreams. Two days of alternate terror and ecstasy must be affecting her brain. She had always prided herself on the practicality of her nature. As a practical woman, how could she believe, even for a moment, that Lord Moreton was ready to count the world well lost for passion? He had told her he desired her, but he had spoken no words of love. He had made no promises of undying devotion. She forced herself to face up to the fact that he had probably made love to a hundred other women. His skill as a lover came from experience, not from the tenderness of his feelings for her. Their love-making had transported her to paradise; that did not mean that Lord Moreton had joined her there.

She felt Paulo's hand tugging at her sodden cape, and she saw that they had actually reached the outskirts of Lisbon. She glanced swiftly towards Lord Moreton, but he did not look at her, and the coldness of despair squeezed a little tighter around her heart.

She scarcely noticed the bustling activity of the city streets as they crossed the western part of the town and arrived at the harbour. She heard a brief, quick cry of triumph from Lord Moreton, and looked up to see their ship still riding at anchor, the British flag blowing proudly in the brisk January breeze.

Paulo grinned and let out a rushing stream of Portuguese, obviously very much pleased with himself and his skill as a guide. Diane smiled, sharing his pleasure, although she was so tired and so numb with cold that she had no energy to celebrate their success with the intensity it deserved.

Lord Moreton, after his one triumphant ex-clamation, retreated again into silence, walking the last few paces along the quay with his face averted both from Paulo and from Diane.

Paulo pulled the donkey to a halt at the ship's side, and a great shout went up from the watching sailors as they recognised Lord Moreton's mud-spattered uniform. Within minutes, their party was surrounded by a swarm of sailors and soldiers, the bright scarlet of their jackets making a welcoming splash of colour against the gloom of the winter afternoon.

A dozen helping hands reached out to assist Diane from the donkey, but she was paralysed by her fatigue. Try as she might, her hands would not loosen their tight hold on the reins, and her legs refused to straighten out and allow her to slide to the ground.

Suddenly she felt Lord Moreton's arms around her waist. 'Hold on to my shoulders,' he said curtly. There was no trace of kindness in his voice, but warmth flowed into her body where he touched her, and her hands instinctively obeyed his command.

'Let me pass, please,' he said, and a pathway through the crowd of soldiers and sailors immediately appeared.

He walked swiftly across the quay and up the narrow gangplank, arriving on board just as his brother and the ship's captain reached the same spot.

'Lord Moreton!' Captain Fortescue exclaimed. 'Thank heaven you have returned! We have been sick with worry ever since we heard about the attack on the Marques's carriage and the murder of his servants!'

Captain Moreton thumped his brother feverishly on the back, his grin stretching almost from one ear to the other. 'Edward, thank God! We have feared everything imaginable! By Jupiter, it's good to see you!'

'It's good to be here. Please let me through, Edward, I must take my wife to her cabin. She is exhausted and half-dead with cold. Her hands were frozen on the reins.'

'I am not cold any longer,' Diane protested. She suddenly realised that she felt so blissfully warm and protected because Lord Moreton was holding her. She stirred within his arms, but his grasp seemed to tighten fractionally around her, preventing her from standing.

'My lord, you should put me down,' she murmured. 'You must be even more exhausted than I am. I have ridden here, but you covered all those weary miles on foot. I can walk to the cabin, my lord.'

'There is no need,' he said shortly. 'You are a very light burden.' He turned to his brother. 'William, please send some female servants to the cabin with soap and hot water and tea for my wife.' He nodded to the ship's captain without waiting for his brother to reply. 'With your permission, Captain Fortescue, I will join you when I have seen to my wife's comfort. I'm sure you will appreciate that she has endured a great deal during the past two days, and that her well-being is my first concern.'

Diane could not hear Captain Fortescue's reply because of the bubble of happiness enveloping her. Lord Moreton had called her his wife. He had made the magic acknowledgment three times. *My wife.* The words echoed in her head as he walked swiftly along the corridor to their cabin. Perhaps, after all, he envisaged some future for them together. She felt almost suffocated with joy.

Once inside their cabin, he placed her gently on the bed, but he turned away so quickly that she had no chance to catch her breath, much less to say anything. He paused in the doorway, his back half-turned towards her. 'I will leave you now, Diane. Whatever you need for your comfort, you have only to ask. I shall instruct the servants to respond to your every need.'

'You will not stay, my lord?' she questioned huskily, hurt by the unexpected abruptness of his departure. He made no response, and she abandoned all consideration of personal pride. 'Please stay with me,' she pleaded softly. 'Do not go for a little while, my lord. We have so much to say to each other.'

'I cannot stay now.' She saw that his knuckles had turned white where he gripped the open door-frame and, before she could say anything further, he had passed through it without another glance in her direction. The door slammed shut, and within a few seconds the last echo of his footsteps had faded into silence.

Her brief moment of euphoria leaked away in unison with his retreating steps. A maid arrived carrying a steaming canister of hot water, followed by another maid bearing a laden tray of refreshments, and Diane was soon lying back in a porcelain bathtub while one of the maids poured scented water through her hair.

The bath revived her aching body but not her aching spirits. The last trace of her optimism faded, dissipated by the expert but impersonal ministrations of the servants. She contrasted the luxury

of her present surroundings with the primitive bedroom in Anna Maria's cottage, and there was no
difficulty in deciding where she would rather have
been. She remembered the touch of her husband's
hands on her shoulders, the feel of his fingers
running through her hair. She remembered the
throb of passion in his voice as he had whispered
that he wanted her. She remembered the leap of
desire in his dark eyes when he had finally possessed her and, even though she tried to shut out the
memory, she remembered the trembling tenderness of his ultimate possession.

The maids wrapped her in soft, warm towels and
shook out the delicate lace of her undergarments.
She sat docilely while they tied the ribbons and
buttoned the buttons on her petticoats and turned
her once again into a jewelled and sparkling lady of
fashion. She stood obediently while they dressed
her in a blue silk and wool afternoon gown and
thought of her foolish hopes for the future, the
hopes that had sustained her through the weary
miles of the journey back to Lisbon. She thought of
her dream of a life spent with her husband in the
peacefulness of an English village. Then she forced
herself to visualise reality: the island of St Helena
where she would spend the rest of her life—alone.
So much for daydreams, she thought cynically, and
closed her eyes to shut in the tears.

When the maids were finally satisfied with her
appearance, they plied her with tea and wafer-thin
slices of bread and butter. Then they summoned
two young subalterns to escort her to Captain
Fortescue's cabin. She was sufficiently restored to

sanity by her bath and all the food to speculate on exactly why the young officers had been assigned to escort her. For her safety? Or to prevent her from running away? In her new mood of cynicism, the latter explanation seemed more likely.

One of the young subalterns tapped on the captain's door, and she heard the command to enter. She went in, noticing vaguely that the cabin was large and pleasantly panelled in some light-stained wood, and that Captain Moreton was standing next to Captain Fortescue. She heard the dismissal of the two young officers and then, despite every one of her good intentions, all her powers of observation became concentrated upon Lord Moreton.

He, like her, had bathed and changed. His two-day growth of beard had been shaven and he now wore an immaculately tailored jacket of dark grey superfine. His linen was impeccably white, his cravat crisply folded, and when he turned to acknowledge her presence she felt as if she was being greeted by an elegant stranger. Lord Moreton, she realised with a bitter sensation of loss, was once again the sardonic, aloof diplomat of the London salons. The loving, teasing, tender man who had shared her bed for the last two nights had vanished without leaving a trace.

'My lady.' If there was any note of personal warmth in his voice, she could not hear it. He inclined his head in a polite acknowledgment of her presence. 'You look much rested.'

Pride kept her voice reasonably level, although pride had unfortunately returned too late to protect her heart. She lifted her chin and stared straight into his eyes. 'You, too, look greatly improved, my lord. I dare say I would not recognise you if we had not known each other in London.'

He smiled. 'The beneficial effects of hot water are amazing, are they not?'

Captain Fortescue cleared his throat with evident impatience. 'Perhaps you would like to sit down, my lady. Lord Moreton has just finished explaining to us how your carriage came to be attacked when you left the Marques's dinner-party.'

Captain Moreton looked at her critically, speaking for the first time. 'Do you have anything to add to my brother's account of the accident, my lady?'

She recognised the blatant hostility in his voice, and with some difficulty managed to prevent herself flinching under the sharpness of his question. 'I don't know,' she replied coolly. 'Since I have no idea what Lord Moreton has already told you.'

'I have told them that we were attacked by a gang of marauding ex-soldiers and that you saved my life,' he said. 'I have told them that if it had not been for your courage while I was unconscious, we would both have been left for dead, along with the Marques's grooms.'

She looked up quickly, aware suddenly of some note of suppressed emotion in Lord Moreton's voice. His eyes were guarded, but she had long since learned to interpret the faint changes in his expression, and she realised with a flash of incredulity that he somehow blamed himself for the success of the brigands' attack.

'You flatter me, my lord!' she said softly. 'You

know that I did almost nothing. It was the sight of your British uniform that saved us both.'

The remoteness of his expression relaxed into a sudden warmth, and he emerged from behind the captain's desk to come and stand beside her. Ignoring the other people in the room, he lifted her hand to his lips. 'We shall not argue about it,' he said huskily. 'We can surely find better things to do with our time.'

She was quite unable to control the leap of hope that set her pulses racing, and she looked at him, knowing that her heart was in her eyes. He took her other hand and pressed it gently against his cheek.

'I have left you to tell Captain Fortescue and my brother about the impersonation that Senhor Carvalho plans. I know you are tired, but try to recall every detail of your meeting with Senhor Carvalho. It will be a big help if you can make your descriptions as precise as possible.'

She recounted everything that she could remember, racking her brains to recall every nuance of the man's voice and every detail of his appearance. Captain Fortescue listened in attentive silence, interjecting occasional quick questions. At last he seemed satisfied that he had extracted every possible piece of relevant information and sat back in his chair with an air of restrained satisfaction.

'Captain Moreton will be given the task of making the arrest,' he said. 'We shall have to alert the governor to the situation, but I shall make as little of it as possible. You know what the governor is like—he suspects murder plots and insurrection at every turn, and news of this plot will confirm all of his worst nightmares. The less said about all this, the better. If Captain Moreton can make the arrest quickly enough, we shall bring Senhor Carvalho back as a prisoner on this very ship. With luck, he may never set foot on shore.'

'And I shall undertake to warn the British and Portuguese Governments about the Marques de Algarve Branca as soon as I get back to London,' Lord Moreton said. 'Unfortunately, I think that he is too powerful a man to be arrested on mere suspicion of being a Napoleonic sympathiser. But his activities can certainly be watched a great deal more closely than they have been in the past.'

'What about Mr Baker?' Diane asked.

Lord Moreton hesitated for a fraction of a second. 'He, too, will have to be dealt with.'

Captain Moreton glanced towards his brother, a touch of defiance in his manner. 'We have already sent a courier to London with a despatch ordering his arrest. He will be deported to France, where the Bourbons will no doubt make him regret that he ever decided to support Napoleon's cause.'

Lord Moreton appeared angry. 'I did not give permission for Mr Baker's arrest,' he said.

'We imagined you to be dead,' his brother replied tersely. 'In the circumstances, we were determined that Baker at least should face up to the consequences of his treachery.'

Lord Moreton's hands tightened their grasp around Diane's fingers, then one arm slipped around her waist. 'I hope this news about your guardian does not distress you too much,' he said quietly.

'No, how could you think it might? I regret that Mr Baker didn't use his talents and his undoubted intelligence more productively. But he was never my friend, and so I have no personal regrets about his deportation.'

Lord Moreton left his arm round Diane's waist as he turned to speak to Captain Fortescue. 'My wife and I have now told you everything we know. If by any chance we should remember some other detail, we shall not hesitate to pass it on to you. We are very tired and, with your permission, we should like to retire. We shall take dinner in our cabin tonight, if you will excuse us from your table.'

Captain Fortescue did not appear completely happy with this arrangement, although he could not, in common courtesy, countermand it. Diane sensed considerable restraint in his manner as he thanked her for her help and wished her a good night's rest after all her adventures. It was obvious, she thought wearily, that the ship's captain was not at all pleased with Diane's sudden transformation from suspect-in-chief to heroine.

'I will come with you to the cabin, Edward,' Captain Moreton said. 'We have a great deal still to discuss.'

'Could it not wait until tomorrow morning?'

Captain Moreton's expression was grim. 'I believe not,' he said. 'I believe there are matters we should talk about right away.'

There was no mistaking the Captain's state of suppressed anger and, as soon as they reached the cabin, he rounded upon his brother. 'Well,

Edward, I understand you plan to leave the ship at first light tomorrow morning.'

'Yes.'

'And what of—Diane?'

Lord Moreton became intensely interested in the patch of inky water visible outside the porthole. 'Naturally, Diane comes with me. She is my wife.'

'Is she?' the Captain said. 'Then I must say she has used these two days of your absence to very good effect. It is true that she is beautiful enough to turn any man's head, and certainly desirable enough to tempt even a connoisseur of women into indiscretion. But have you stopped to consider, Edward, that she is also a traitor to our country?'

Lord Moreton paled. 'If you were not my brother, William, you would not live long enough to repeat any of those remarks.'

Diane gave a small cry of distress and interposed herself between the two men. 'Ah, dear God, do not look at each other in such a fashion! Please don't force me to add responsibility for your enmity to all my other sins. My lord . . . I beg of you . . .'

The sheen of fury faded from Lord Moreton's eyes and, after a moment's evident struggle, he produced a slight smile. 'I think I have spent too much time among thieves and brigands recently. I am beginning to act like my captors. William, I'm sorry. I have not slept for two nights, and today I walked many more miles than I care to think about. By the time I returned to the ship, I was so exhausted that I could barely stand.'

'Is *that* why you left me so abruptly?' Diane exclaimed. 'Because you were tired?'

'Yes.' He lifted his shoulders in a self-deprecating shrug. 'I seemed to have spent a great deal of time over the past few days fainting into your arms. For once, I wanted to get out of your sight before I keeled over.'

'You mean that, when you left me, you fainted!'

His expression became even more rueful. 'I'm afraid so. It is becoming something of a habit with me recently.'

'I would remind you that we still have some important matters to discuss,' Captain Moreton interjected stiffly.

Lord Moreton sighed. 'Yes, we do, but frankly I am not in the mood for giving you complex explanations and justifications for my behaviour. Could you bring yourself to accept my apology? And to accept my word that I was mistaken about Diane and her role in Mr Baker's schemes? I assure you that, without her help, Senhor Carvalho's plans would never have been unmasked.'

'Perhaps I can accept that she is not a traitor,' the Captain said stiffly. 'But what of her role in your life, Edward? How is she to fit into our family? You claim her now as your wife, but have you already forgotten that she was once *my* fiancée?'

Lord Moreton grimaced uncertainly, and to Diane's astonishment she saw an embarrassed blush creep up and stain his cheeks. 'There is nothing I can say in defence of my actions except that I fell in love with Diane the first time I saw her. I married her, and despite all the clever reasons I gave myself to justify that marriage, I knew from the first that there was no real chance I would ever allow the marriage to be annulled. I love her, William. I love her more than I believed I could love any woman, and my life will not be worth living if she is not a part of it.'

'You may remember that I once told you more or less the same thing about my own feelings for her.'

A hint of wry laughter mingled with the embarrassment in Lord Moreton's eyes. 'But there is one important difference, William,' he said. 'I have never claimed to be in love before. With you, it is a monthly occurrence.'

The faintest of smiles chased away some of the anger lingering in the Captain's expression. 'Well, as for that, I think I have finally learned my lesson,' he said. 'I can assure you that I do not plan to fall in love again for a very long time.'

'In that case, might I persuade you to wish us happiness?'

The Captain glanced towards Diane. 'Do you love him?' he asked bluntly.

She drew in a deep, harsh breath, not daring to look at Lord Moreton. 'Yes, I love him,' she admitted shakily. 'I love him with everything that is in me, with every part of me that is capable of loving.'

The Captain dropped his gaze. 'In all the months that we knew each other, you never once said that you loved me. I think I always suspected, in my heart of hearts, that you didn't speak the words because you didn't want to tell a lie.'

He turned abruptly to his brother and took his hand in a quick, firm hand-shake. 'I wish you both every joy in your married life,' he said. 'Perhaps I shall have a godson to be named after me by the time I return from St Helena. At the very least, I expect a niece to dandle on my knee.'

He did not wait for his brother to reply, neither did he look again in Diane's direction. He walked out, leaving them alone in the candle-lit cabin.

They stared at each other across two feet of carpeted floor that suddenly seemed wider than a mountain abyss.

Lord Moreton turned his attention to re-lighting one of the candles, and he seemed totally absorbed in the simple task of trimming the wick.

'Did you mean what you told my brother?' he asked finally, still without turning to look at her.

'That I loved you?' she asked. 'Yes, I meant it.'

She heard the swift intake of his breath as he crossed the room and swept her into his arms. 'Oh God!' he said unsteadily. 'I do not deserve your love, but I have so longed to hear you confess it. Diane, can you possibly forgive me for the way I treated you when we first met?'

'There is nothing to forgive,' she said. 'On the contrary, it is I who should ask for your forgiveness.'

His arms tightened fiercely around her, crushing her against his chest as he kissed her with a passion that left them both on fire with longing. He pulled her to the bed, his hands shaking with urgency as he traced the soft slope of her shoulders and the delicate swell of her breast.

'Does that mean you will come back with me to Wellespont?' he murmured. 'Do you think you could become accustomed to spending your life as the wife of an English country gentleman?'

She longed to say Yes, so that she could give herself up to the mindless joy of his caresses, but her conscience would not permit such an easy escape.

'Edward, I don't think you have considered what you are suggesting. Are you sure you wish to acknowledge our marriage? Perhaps it is not too late to have it annulled. Remember . . .' She swallowed hard. 'Remember that my father betrayed your country, the country which gave him refuge when he fled from the Terror. And I . . . I was so desperate to win my father's love that I agreed to help Mr Baker. I thought that if—just once—I could do precisely as my father wished, it would make up for all those years when I had failed him.'

Lord Moreton smoothed her hair away from her forehead. 'You did not fail your father,' he said. 'The failure was all on the other side.'

'He wanted a son,' she said and it was an overwhelming relief to make the simple confession aloud. 'My mother died producing me, and then I was only a female.'

'Thank heaven for that,' Lord Moreton murmured, pushing her back against the pillows. His hands roamed enticingly over her curves and she felt her skin dissolve into a hazy mass of tingling nerve endings. She forced her brain into action, while it still retained some vestigial power of rational thought. She put her hands over his, stilling their seductive movements.

'My lord, there are other problems. Think of them! What will your neighbours say if you marry the daughter of an émigré French count? They will not want you to marry a foreigner. I am sure they have at least a dozen eligible local girls already looked out for your inspection.'

'They will say I have married you for your money,' he said with a grin. 'Did you not know that you have a great deal more money than I do, and that Wellespont is sadly in need of some extra cash?'

'My money cannot buy forgiveness from your family,' she said.

'I wouldn't be so sure of that. It is a very great deal of money, you know.'

She would not be diverted by his teasing. 'My lord, your family consider me a traitor—they think of me as the woman who conspired to set Napoleon free. They will never accept me as your wife, whatever the size of my dowry.'

He kissed the side of her mouth in an effort to silence her protests, but when he saw that she was genuinely troubled he reached out and curled her tenderly into the curve of his shoulder. 'You have already met my mother,' he said with a tiny smile. 'So you should realise that she cares little for the political convictions of anybody born during the last two thousand years. Unless your sympathies should happen to be for the wrong side in the Peloponnesian Wars, I doubt if we need to anticipate any trouble.'

It was almost impossible to feel worried about anything when he held her so tightly against his heart. 'But which is the wrong side?' she asked, nestling more comfortably against the muscled strength of his chest. 'Did they not kill each other with equal ferocity for no very good reason?'

'Tut, tut, my dear, now you are truly speaking treason. The Spartans are the wrong side, of course, although pray do not ask me why. Just remember to cheer every time my mother mentions Athens, and she will be quite willing to ignore your minor indiscretions with regard to Monsieur Napoleon.'

She could not help smiling. 'Unfortunately, your sister and her husband don't share your mother's obsession with Classical Greece. They will care very much about what I have done.'

'You have foiled a clever plot to set free Napoleon. Without your help, the plan might well have succeeded. So far as I know, that is cause for congratulation, not for complaint.'

He tilted her chin up in his hands, brushing his thumbs gently down the side of her face. 'Enough of this nonsense, my love. If you will not have me, you must say so. But don't bring in my mother and my sister and my poor old brother-in-law as excuses. I shall never accept them.'

It was becoming increasingly impossible to re-member why she ought to resist him, but she forced out a final question. 'What of your brother? You have always been such good friends, I could not bear to come between you.'

'Diane, we both know that my brother will have fallen in love at least half a dozen times before he returns from St Helena. You were not the love of his life, and he will soon know that for himself.'

Diane looked up into her husband's eyes, and the

depth of feeling she saw there caused her heart to race and her pulses to pound. 'You are the love of my life,' she whispered. 'I want to love you.'

Lord Moreton did not respond to her in words. He flung himself off the bed and walked to the cabin door. He locked it and threw the bolt across before turning round to face her, a tender smile twisting the corners of his mouth.

'We have the whole night ahead of us, my lady. Show me exactly what you mean.'

Mills & Boon

Your chance to step into the past Take 2 Books FREE

Discover a world long vanished. An age of chivalry and intrigue, powerful desires and exotic locations. Read about true love found by soldiers and statesmen, princesses and serving girls. All written as only Mills & Boon's top-selling authors know how. Become a regular reader of Mills & Boon Masquerade Historical Romances and enjoy 4 superb, new titles every two months, plus a whole range of special benefits: your very own personal membership card entitles you to a regular free newsletter packed with recipes, competitions, exclusive book offers plus other bargain offers and big cash savings.

AND an Introductory FREE GIFT for YOU.
Turn over the page for details.

**Fill in and send this coupon back today
and we will send you**

2 Introductory
Historical Romances
FREE

At the same time we will reserve a subscription to
Mills & Boon Masquerade Historical Romances for
you. Every two months you will receive Four new,
superb titles delivered direct to your door. You
don't pay extra for delivery. Postage and packing is
always completely free. There is no obligation or
commitment – you only receive books for as long as
you want to.

**Just fill in and post the coupon today to MILLS & BOON
READER SERVICE, FREEPOST, P.O. BOX 236, CROYDON,
SURREY CR9 9EL.**

**Please Note:- READERS iN SOUTH AFRICA write to
Mills & Boon, Postbag X3010,
Randburg 2125, S. Africa.**

FREE BOOKS CERTIFICATE

**To: Mills & Boon Reader Service, FREEPOST, P.O. Box 236,
Croydon, Surrey CR9 9EL.**

Please send me, free and without obligation, two Masquerade Historical Romances, and
reserve a Reader Service Subscription for me. If I decide to subscribe I shall receive,
following my free parcel of books, four new Masquerade Historical Romances every two
months for £5.00, post and packing free. If I decide not to subscribe, I shall write to you
within 10 days. The free books are mine to keep in any case. I understand that I may cancel
my subscription at any time simply by writing to you. I am over 18 years of age.

Please write in BLOCK CAPITALS.

Signature _____

Name _____

Address _____

_____ Post code _____

SEND NO MONEY — TAKE NO RISKS.

Please don't forget to include your Postcode.

Remember, postcodes speed delivery. Offer applies in UK only and is not valid
to present subscribers. Mills & Boon reserve the right to exercise discretion in
granting membership. If price changes are necessary you will be notified,
4M   Offer expires December 24th 1984.

EP9N